CORNISH QUEST

Virginia (Ginny) Shaw comes to Cornwall to research her family history and realises her relationship with Phil is over. She meets the charismatic Greg and gets drawn into his world of sea and surfing. At a fancy-dress party, however, their friendship is tested when Ginny upsets Greg by discovering his hidden secret. And then she is wrongfully accused of theft. Can they be reconciled? And can true love and happiness be theirs?

JANET THOMAS

CORNISH QUEST

Complete and Unabridged

LINFORD
Leicester

First published in Great Britain in 2008

First Linford Edition
published 2009

British Library CIP Data

Thomas, Janet, *1936* Oct. 24–
    Cornish quest- -(Linford romance library)
    1. Cornwall (England: County)- -Fiction.
    2. Love stories.
    3. Large type books.
    I. Title II. Series
    823.9′2–dc22

ISBN 978–1–84782–797–5

Published by
F. A. Thorpe (Publishing)
Anstey, Leicestershire

Set by Words & Graphics Ltd.
Anstey, Leicestershire
Printed and bound in Great Britain by
T. J. International Ltd., Padstow, Cornwall

This book is printed on acid-free paper

'Who Was My Mother?'

'Well, a fine holiday this is turning out to be, I must say!' I jumped as Phil's irritated voice behind me broke my concentration. Hitting the 'save' button on my laptop, I swivelled round from the microfilm reader to face him.

'Oh, Phil, I shan't be much longer, really,' I said with what I hoped was a soothing smile, 'but keep your voice down a bit — this is a library, remember.'

'As if I could forget.' He growled. 'You spend long enough in here.'

I bit my lip to hold back the sharp retort that hovered, and instead said, 'Well, we can go on to St. Ives now, just as we planned.'

'We 'planned' to be there two hours ago, if you remember,' he snapped, turning away and tapping an impatient foot.

'I do know,' I said to his angry back

1

as I rewound the film, then picked up my belongings. 'And I'm sorry, but when this great lead came up I just had to follow it through.'

'Did you find what you were after?' Greg, the library assistant, came towards us and I handed him the reel of film.

'I've made a very good start,' I replied, smiling up at him. Blond as a Viking with a tan to die for and all of six feet two or three, he towered over both Phil and myself.

'Thanks so much for all your help — I'll be back again soon.'

'You're very welcome — and I'll look forward to seeing you then.' He raised a hand in farewell and strode away.

'Huh — you two seem very friendly,' Phil said, glowering at me.

Surprised at this hint of jealousy, I suppressed a smile.

'Yes,' I replied. 'He's a nice chap — very friendly and helpful. Not a bit stuffy like some archivists.'

We were outside the building and

walking back to the car when I apologised again for taking longer than I'd meant to.

'I thought you would understand, Phil,' I added, threading my arm through his. 'After all, it's what we agreed to do when we decided to come down to Cornwall,' I said.

Looking directly at him, I could see how stormy his face still was.

'Remember?' I cajoled. 'I would try to trace my family forebears and you would go off and do your bird watching, photography and all that while I was working. Then we would spend the rest of our time together.'

He snorted. 'That was before I found out how much time you were going to take up with this stupid idea, Virginia,' he snapped, glowering down at me, his use of my full name a sure sign of how put-out he was. 'Plus, it's hardly stopped raining since we've been here — '

'Well, that's hardly my fault, is it?' I chipped in, and heard the sharp edge to my voice. I sighed heavily. We were rowing again. It was happening more and more, and not only just recently.

I did a quick recap over the past few months and, yes, the cracks had been there long before we'd come away. It was one reason why we'd come on holiday. The other was totally for my own concerns.

⋆　⋆　⋆

The idea had come to me one winter evening when we were curled up on the sofa in my flat in London. Phil was switching from channel to channel with the remote, trying to find something worth watching, and I was sifting through a pile of books, preparing tomorrow's work for my year-three class at the local primary. Mother's Day was coming up and I was thinking of giving them a craft lesson — they could make paper flowers or something — and that's when I had the idea.

'Phil,' I said, shifting the pile of books

from my lap to the low table at my elbow, 'you know I've told you that I never knew my parents?'

He nodded and gave a grunt, his attention still on the screen. 'Because they were killed in a car smash when you were a few weeks old. But that's all you've told me about them.'

'Well, when Grandma officially adopted me and decided to bring me up, I was taken to Birmingham to live with her and my dad's family, and I never knew much about any relatives on my mother's side, except for some vague remarks that they came from Cornwall.'

'I don't think the two families could have been very friendly, actually.' I nibbled a thumbnail as I cast my mind back. 'Grandma would never talk much about them, or my mother, and when I asked questions she would always brush me off and change the subject.'

'So what's all this leading up to, Ginny?' Phil turned to face me, the remote poised in one hand. 'Because this looks like being a good thriller and

I don't want to miss the beginning of it.'

'Oh, never mind,' I said. 'We can talk later if that's the way you feel,' and I moved to get up.

His brow furrowed. 'There's no need to snap like that,' he replied. 'Surely you don't begrudge me a bit of telly after I've been slogging away in the office all day, do you?' Phil was a chartered accountant.

'But I didn't snap!' I exclaimed, and meant it. 'It's just the way you took it.'

He laid the remote down on the arm of his chair, took off his glasses and pinched the bridge of his nose. A cowlick of black hair drooped across his forehead and he brushed it back with impatience.

'Sorry, Gin,' he conceded, 'I guess I'm just tired — I've had a hard day.'

I sat down again and reached for his hand. 'That's OK,' I murmured, making an effort to come halfway to meet him, although these spats were happening more and more often lately and, if I was honest, I was becoming less and less inclined to try to resolve them.

'Actually,' I ventured, 'it leads in to what I wanted to say. You need a holiday. And so do I. It's nearly the end of the Easter term, so why don't you take what's still owing to you from last year, before you have to forget it, and we could go away for a couple of weeks? Somewhere relaxing.'

'Hmm.' His forehead puckered as he replaced his spectacles, and his toffee-brown eyes were expressionless. 'Abroad, you mean?'

'Not exactly . . . '

I reached across him for the remote and clicked off the meaningless babble.

'You don't mind, do you?' I asked. 'I can't talk or think over that.'

Phil shook his head. 'Not really. I'm too tired to concentrate anyway. What were you saying?'

'I'd like to go down to Cornwall,' I replied. 'I've been looking at these brochures — here.' I picked up a pile of leaflets and waved them under his nose. 'I'm sure you'd like it. There's beautiful scenery for your photography, and all kinds of wildlife. It looks absolutely lovely. And — ' I paused and took in a breath, wondering how he would take my next remark ' — I would like to put some of my time into trying to trace my mother's family.'

He gave me a surprised look. 'Family history? That's pretty dull stuff, surely?' he said disparagingly. 'What's the point in rooting about in the past looking up people you never knew and who died years ago?'

My mouth drooped with disappointment. Of course he wouldn't understand. Why should he? I ran a hand through my hair and sighed.

Phil's roots on both sides were firmly grounded in South London. He had a phalanx of aunts, uncles, cousins and countless extended family members who knew exactly who they were and where they belonged. He had never known what it was like to feel that a part of him was missing. He could have no idea what it was like to feel this blank space which ached to be filled with people, deceased or not.

He must have noticed my glum expression, because one arm came round my shoulders and he gave me a squeeze.

'If it's important to you, then of course that's what we'll do,' he said, dropping a kiss on the end of my nose. 'So cheer up, put the sparkle back in those lovely blue eyes of yours and let's have a cup of coffee. We can sift through some of those pamphlets at the same time. How about that, eh?'

Cornwall

So that's how we came to be staying in a holiday cottage, actually the renovated barn of an old farm, looking out over the north Cornish coast through the slanting silver drizzle which had been the hallmark of our visit so far. Three days in and we'd hardly seen the sun.

I didn't really mind for myself as I was quite happy doing my search in the library and the records office, but I was well aware of how frustrated Phil was. He was standing with his back to me now, staring gloomily out over the bay. A family of four, all of them sporting colourful cagoules, went past on the cliff path below us, obviously determined to go to the beach, drizzle or not.

With a sigh, I closed my notebook and packed away my work. Phil's moody presence was making concentration impossible.

I really ought to be sharing more of my time with him, I thought with a slight twinge of guilt. But when I'd first thought of coming down here I'd had visions of me getting on with my work while he went out with his camera. I hadn't reckoned on this abysmal weather thwarting that plan so completely.

Just then, thank goodness, a shaft of pale sunlight — a weak and watery thing but sunlight nonetheless — poked its fingers through the haze and gently began to tear it into ribbons of pearly gauze.

'It's clearing up, Phil, look — actually clearing!' I said, joining him at the window. 'Wonderful — let's go for a walk, shall we?'

A few minutes later we were on our way. The tide was receding and the long stretch of amber sand curving away into the distance was newly washed, dotted here and there with shallow pools, which were beginning to sparkle and shine in the strengthening sun. Three miles of golden sands, the holiday brochure stated proudly, all the way from Gwithian and Godrevy at its eastern boundary round to Hayle and St. Ives in the west.

The sun had brought out all the holidaymakers like us who had been cooped up for too long in their caravans and chalets, waiting for the weather to clear. Shrieking children were paddling at the edge of the sea, while farther out the swelling waves were dotted with the black shapes of surfers looking remarkably like the seals which frequented this coast, and seeming almost as agile.

'Wait, Phil,' I called as I stopped to take off my sandals. 'I'm going to paddle like the children!' I pushed my cropped trousers higher up my legs. 'Why don't you come in, too?'

He shrugged and made no move to take off his trainers.

'I'm OK as I am,' he replied and we strolled on, me splashing at the very edge of the water and him remaining on the firm, damp sand not far away.

One of the black-clad surfers was emerging from the waves as our paths crossed. As he peeled back his hood and tucked his board under his arm he did a double take.

'Ginny!' he said. 'Well, hello, this is a surprise! And — er — Phil, isn't it?'

'Greg!' I exclaimed, recognising him. 'So you're a surfer? I hardly recognised you.'

He grinned and, seating himself on a flat rock nearby, patted the space beside him.

'Come and join me while I warm up in the sun,' he said with another flash of gleaming white teeth. 'Oh, yes, I'll say I am — I can't get enough of surfing. I spend all my spare time down here.' So that would account for the tan, I thought.

'It seems ever so skilful to me,' I said, 'the way they keep their balance and follow the wave all the way in — like that chap there.' I pointed.

'Do you like the water?' Greg asked and I nodded.

'I love to swim,' I replied, 'but that's all. I don't think surfing would be for me.'

'It's easy enough to learn,' he replied. 'You must start off in a small way and the more you practise the better at it you become.'

I nodded. 'I suppose so — but there's not a lot of scope for that in South London, as you can imagine!'

'How about you, Phil?' Greg turned towards him, plainly trying to include him.

Phil raised a shoulder. 'Oh, I'm a good enough swimmer,' he said as he gazed out to sea, 'when I choose to. But personally I prefer a proper pool to the ocean. It seems more . . . civilised somehow.'

I heard Greg's indrawn breath and saw how his brows rose. Then I glanced at Phil. Had he meant the remark as the calculated insult it had sounded, or was he just trying to put Greg down? Either way, it seemed totally uncalled for and I glared at him, but his attention was still on the sea and he wouldn't meet my eyes.

Greg had risen lithely to his feet and was picking up his surfboard.

'Well, I'd better go — I'm on duty,' he remarked. 'I'll see you around, I expect.' He raised a hand and began to make his way towards the lifesavers' headquarters, an imposing purpose-built structure at the top of the beach. So, he must be a beach lifeguard; obviously a voluntary one because of his job.

'I spend all my spare time down here,' he had said, hadn't he? So that was why.

Phil's voice cut in sharply on my thoughts. 'Are you going to sit there all day, Virginia? I thought we were meant to be having a walk.'

I looked at him as I jumped up, and saw that his mouth was set in a firm line of disapproval. He *is* jealous, I thought, and stifled a hoot of laughter. But it wasn't really funny at all. His thin face was set and the jutting jaw as hard as the granite cliffs above us.

However, as the sunshine brought out more and more of the brilliant colours of sea and sky, I saw him reach for his camera. A good sign.

By the time we had climbed the cliff and the magnificent sweep of the bay was spread out at our feet, his mood had improved, and soon he was happily checking the light and firing off dozens of shots, lost in his own little world, and *I* was waiting for *him*.

★　★　★

I couldn't wait to get back to the library next morning, to follow the lead I had had to abandon when time had run out on my last visit.

Fortunately the day was another fine one, so I took the car and headed for town, leaving Phil happily preparing to walk the cliffs and dunes in search of the peregrine falcons, fulmars and buzzards which apparently were to be found there, as well as several species of gull which, to be honest, all looked alike to me.

I glanced around for Greg when I arrived but he wasn't about, so I was given the tape I needed by another assistant, and was soon immersed in the past.

According to the census returns which I was studying, my mother had been born in 1940, to a farm labourer, and had been the youngest of six daughters. So presumably the family had been quite poor. But I had aunts — and presumably cousins — that I had never known existed!

Following the elation of this, I felt a stab of pain for so many wasted years, and anger at my grandmother for keeping it all from me, for it would take a lifetime to trace these relatives now. Being female, they would doubtless have married and changed their names long ago.

So, what *did* I know? I knew from their marriage certificate that my parents had wed in 1970, and I had been born in 1973, the year both my parents had died in the accident when I had been six months old.

So, what had happened in my mother's early life to earn her such disapproval from my grandmother?

I nibbled my pen and was staring into space when a voice came at my elbow and I turned to see Greg at my side.

'Penny for them?' he said with a smile. 'You looked as if you were miles away.'

I smiled back as I looked up into his laughing face. 'I was,' I replied. 'I'm a bit stuck with this. I don't know what to do next.'

'Well now, what's the problem?' he asked. 'Maybe I can help.'

He bent over me and I felt his warm breath on the back of my neck, which sent a little quiver down the whole length of my spine. He smelled pleasantly of soap and after-shave and crisply laundered denim shirt.

I told him the whole story and he nibbled a thumbnail as he stared at the screen in thought.

'Hmm,' he said at last. 'You've got nothing more to go on? I suppose you haven't any — for example — diaries of hers? Letters, perhaps, that might give you a clue?' He turned towards me and shook his head. 'But I suppose that's a silly question.'

'Afraid so,' I replied. 'The only things of hers that have come down to me are a few pieces of jewellery, and this.'

I rummaged in the inside pocket of my shoulder bag and pulled out a tiny object in a velvet-lined box that I always carried with me.

'There's this little brooch with her initial on it — you see?' I opened the box and passed it over to him. 'But that's all. It's so precious to me that I take it with me wherever I go.'

Greg took the brooch carefully out of the box and laid it in the palm of his hand, then walked across to the window and held it up to the light. He scrutinised it for several minutes, turning it over and looking at it from all sides, before strolling back to where I was sitting.

'This is really interesting, Ginny,' he remarked as our eyes met, 'more so than I think you realise.'

I raised an eyebrow. 'Oh? How do you mean?'

Greg pulled up a spare chair and sat down at my side.

'You see this letter 'C' here?' He pointed a long slim finger and I nodded.

'Yes, that was her initial. Her name was Caroline — they called her Carrie.'

Greg slowly shook his head. 'Maybe so, but that's not the reason it's on this brooch.' He laid it down on the desk and sat back, folding his arms. 'That 'C' is a special one, Ginny. The way it's designed, sloping to the right like that, with the gilt crown on top, is instantly recognisable to anyone living in this district.'

I gaped at him. 'It is?' I felt my eyes widen as I gave him all my attention.

'Oh, yes.' Greg nodded. 'You see, it's

the crest, or logo, or whatever you might call it, of a large firm of local engineers. They were called Chenoweth, and for many years were the largest employer around here. Originally they manufactured rock drills for the mines, and other machinery, and during the war they turned to munitions.'

'Really?' My brows rose even higher and my heart began to thump. 'So do you think she might have worked there?'

Greg gave a slow smile and replied, 'Almost certainly, I should say. These things were handed out to the employees to wear as a badge to encourage pride in the firm, and also, of course, it was a good marketing ploy for Chenoweths — free advertising for them as well. So there you are.' He handed me back the little brooch and I gazed at it as if seeing it for the first time, before carefully replacing it in its box and burying it in my bag again.

'Thank you so much for that,' I said

to Greg, 'that's really exciting — the first lead I've had. My father was an engineer in Birmingham — perhaps Chenoweth's was where they first met.'

Then I sighed and spread my hands as I added, 'But it still doesn't tell me why she was ostracised by my father's family.'

'Ah.' Greg thought for a bit as the muted voices of other readers and the members of staff going about their business made a backdrop of quiet 'busyness' in the large room.

He looked over his shoulder.

'I'll have to go in a minute,' he remarked, 'there's a queue building up — '

I came back to earth with a bump and turned to face him. 'Oh, of course. I've already taken up more than my fair share of your time.'

'Not at all,' he replied as he pushed back his chair. 'But what I think you could do next,' he added, 'is to glance through the local newspapers for those years, just in case there's something there. It's a bit of a long shot, but if there was ever some kind of scandal, say at the works, and your mother was involved in it, it would have been reported and made the news. They were a pretty prestigious firm.'

I knew my face had fallen at the thought of sifting through piles of yellowing newspapers, and Greg must have noticed because he smiled as he looked down at me and said, 'We've got those on microfilm as well, if you're interested.'

Relieved, I stood up and returned the smile.

'In that case, great, yes, I will.' I glanced at my watch. 'But I must make an appointment for another day. I have to go now.'

'Phil waiting for you, is he?' Greg quirked an eyebrow and our eyes met in mutual understanding. His were intensely blue, and his eyelashes were tipped with little bits of gold . . .

I nodded and hurriedly gathered my things together, then, thanking him again, I left the building.

* ★ *

'Did you get some good photos?' I asked Phil later that evening as I was putting together a meal in the small kitchen of the cottage. He had been looking very pleased with himself when I arrived back, so I presumed he'd had a good day, too.

'Yes, I should say so — fantastic!' he replied, running a hand through his hair as he straightened up from the floor where he had been on his knees in front of the TV, fiddling about with wires and connections.

'I'll run through them with you after dinner. I'm dying to see them on the big screen myself.'

I'd tried to get my head around the intricacies of the digital camera, but apart from pointing and clicking, which I could manage, I had no idea how it worked.

I made a simple meal of steaks and salad and we sat outside on the little patio to eat it and watch the sun sink in the western sky in a blaze of flame and apricot which hinted at another fine day to come tomorrow.

Around us the undulating sand dunes rose, topped with bleached grasses dipping and waving in the breeze off the sea, and on a little round island nearby sat a gleaming white-painted lighthouse, testament to the dangers lurking beneath the surface of this idyllic place.

I waited for Phil to ask me how my day had been, but he obviously wasn't going to, so I said, 'I had a good day, too. You know that brooch of my mother's?'

'Uh-mm,' Phil replied with his mouth full.

I told him the full story and finished, 'So Greg suggested going through the old newspapers to see if I can come up with anything there.'

Phil gave a sardonic snort. 'Oh, really, Virginia, haven't you spent enough time on this wild-goose chase already?' He stabbed his fork into a tomato and held it poised as he glared at me. 'And all you've found out is that your mother worked for this defunct firm, donkey's years ago? Be realistic, for goodness' sake.'

He waved a pointing finger at me. 'How long do you think you'll have to spend in that stuffy library to read twenty years' worth of old papers? Have you thought about that? Days, weeks, maybe months. At the very least it'll take up the rest of our holiday . . . '

He went on and on about 'flogging a dead horse' and my 'obsession', while I ceased to listen and sat there miserably thinking in spite of myself that he might actually be right. It was highly likely that I *would* end up with absolutely nothing to show for my time. And the time factor was certainly a valid point. We only had a fortnight in Cornwall; a week of that was gone already, and we'd hardly been anywhere.

I felt my mouth droop as a wave of disappointment washed over me. I had expected so much, and it was hard to face up to the realisation that I might never find out what I wanted to know.

I pushed my plate back and rose to clear the dishes.

'OK,' I said with a sigh, 'just leave it, you've made your point. Let's go and see those photos of yours over coffee, shall we?'

He brightened immediately, and for the rest of the evening was the old Phil, kind and considerate and loving, while I tried to silence the small voice inside my head that told me, yes, of course he was — he'd got his own way, hadn't he? It was an unattractive character trait that was becoming more and more familiar to me.

I could hardly insist on going back to the library now without causing a full-blown row between us. And besides not wanting to ruin the rest of our holiday, I'd actually lost the heart to even attempt checking newspapers.

Greg's Idea

The next day was a Saturday, as fine as the sunset had predicted, and the beaches were swarming with local families as well as holidaymakers like us, all determined to make the most of the sunshine while it lasted.

I had been stretched out on a towel in a sheltered nook at the base of the cliff, sunbathing, while Phil, who was sitting beside me leaning against a flat rock, had buried himself in a tome about photography, which he'd picked up in a second-hand book shop somewhere. It was getting a bit too hot for comfort, though, and I sat up, tipping back my floppy straw hat to look around.

The sea was rolling in gentle waves on to the soft sand not far from where we were sitting, and it didn't take me long to make up my mind.

'I'm going for a swim to cool off, Phil,' I remarked. 'Do you want to come?'

He looked up and pushed his sunglasses up to his hairline as he thought about it.

Then, 'No-o,' he drawled, 'I'm quite happy here. This is a good book. You go on.'

I shrugged. 'OK,' I replied, and rose to my feet.

The sand was firm and damp as I walked down to the sea, and the small pools which I splashed through on the way were as warm as bath water, which gave me no warning of how cold the sea itself would feel in contrast. I gasped, all the breath leaving my body in shock as a large wave knocked me over and plunged me into its green and salty depths. But it was exciting and exhilarating and I was laughing as I bobbed to the surface like a cork and shook the water out of my eyes.

Not far from me as I drifted towards the beach I noticed a group of young people tossing a ball to one another and alternately swimming and splashing to retrieve it. Then I saw the wind take it and head it my way, and without thinking I put up a hand and caught it. I was preparing to toss it back when one of them detached himself from the group and came wading towards me. I recognised him instantly — that blond head was unmistakable — and I felt a stab of pleasure.

'Greg!' I called and waved.

White teeth gleamed in his tanned face as he gave a huge grin and waved back, pushing his way through the waist-high water between us.

He was wearing red swim shorts, and shining beads of water were pouring from his broad shoulders down over his long lean torso. He slicked his wet hair back from his eyes as another wave caught him as we met.

'Ginny!' he exclaimed, as we both fought to keep our balance against the surge. 'Wow — it's a bit rough today,' he shouted to be heard above the roar of the waves.

'Lovely, though,' I called back. 'Here's your ball — catch!'

I tossed it the short distance between us and he effortlessly fielded it, then jerked his head towards the group.

'Come and join in?' he asked.

I hesitated, shading my eyes with a hand and looking back along the beach towards Phil, but he hadn't moved and his eyes were still fixed on his book. So, why not?

'I'd love to,' I replied, and we sloshed our way back towards the three others who were waiting in the shallows and regarding me with interest. Greg made the introductions.

'This is Lisa — ' He indicated a slim brunette in a bikini which left little to the imagination. ' — Tony,' a bearded, broad-shouldered hunk ' — and Janine,' who was almost as short and round as the ball they were playing with.

'We're all lifeguards,' Greg explained. 'I'm on holiday myself now for a couple of weeks, so I'll be down here most days. So — *catch!*' He hurled the ball at

31

me with no warning, but fortunately my reflexes were quick enough and I didn't make a fool of myself by dropping it.

Soon we had an energetic game going with much shouting and laughter and I found I was really enjoying myself.

After a while, exhausted, we all trooped up the beach and collapsed on the soft dry sand above the tide line. However, I was feeling a pang of guilt at having abandoned Phil. He must be worrying by now as I'd been gone so long. For all he knew, I could still be in the water and maybe in trouble.

When I'd got my breath back I said all this to Greg and reluctantly said goodbye. To my surprise he could almost have been reading my mind because he rose to his feet as well.

'I'll stroll back with you,' he remarked casually, 'to say hello to Phil and explain to him how I've been leading you astray!'

Phil looked up with a face like thunder when he saw us coming, so that I was very glad that Greg was by my side.

'You took your time, I must say,' Phil remarked, his eyes raking over us. 'Had to be rescued by the lifeguard, did you?'

Greg laughed off the remark as if it had really been meant as the joke it seemed to be, but I knew from the edge to his tone that Phil was far from amused.

'Oh, the water was wonderful — though pretty cold!' I replied with a laugh, reaching for a towel to rub at my hair. 'Then I met Greg and his friends and we warmed up with a ball-game in the shallows. It was good fun — you should have come along.'

I sat down on the dry white sand and Greg perched on a rock nearby.

'I've been thinking, Phil,' he said, 'that maybe you and Ginny would like to come out with us tomorrow. We're taking the boat round to Seal Cove — you're interested in wildlife, aren't you? You could get some good shots of them. They're fascinating creatures when you see them in their natural haunts.'

I noticed Phil's expression spark with interest and waited tactfully for him to reply. Me, I was over the moon at the idea, but instead of jumping in right away to say so, for once I managed to hold my tongue and wait.

At last Phil nodded and said in measured tones, 'Hmm, that does sound interesting — although we did have other plans for tomorrow . . . '

We had no such thing and I turned to Phil and raised my eyebrows in amazement.

He caught my glance and hastily added, ' . . . but I suppose we could postpone them. How do you feel about it, Ginny?'

'I'd *love* to,' I replied with enthusiasm. 'I've never *seen* a live seal.'

I looked up at Greg with a broad grin and our eyes met as he smiled back. He didn't exactly wink but I was sure he was perfectly aware of the silent exchange between Phil and me and was highly amused by it.

'Great,' he replied. 'We're meeting at

the harbour at ten. Bring a packed lunch. Oh, and something warm to wear — it can get very cold out at sea.' He stretched lazily then rose to his feet with that easy lithe grace I'd noticed before. 'I'd better be getting back,' he remarked. 'I'll see you in the morning. It should be a nice day, according to the forecast.'

★ ★ ★

And it was. The sun was already warm on my back as we assembled on the cobbled quay. I leaned both arms on the railing, sniffing the pure air, which brought with it the crisp tang of salt and seaweed. Bearing in mind what Greg had said, I was wearing my jeans with a T-shirt and a lightweight pink jumper, and had tied a hooded jacket round my waist. Phil, typically, had insisted that he would be all right in Bermudas and a striped rugby top, so I shrugged and left him to it.

Greg made the introductions again,

but as well as Lisa, Janine and Tony, there was another, older man with them today.

'This is John from the Cornish Environment Trust. He's coming out to monitor the seals,' he said. 'Some of you will know that there's been a bit of concern lately as several dead animals have been found washed up on the beaches.'

There were various nods and murmurs of assent all round.

'So I'm combining work with a day out,' John added in his broad Scots accent as he ran a hand through his thick greying hair. 'We think there may be a virus among them. I'll have to go ashore and check, but I'm afraid you won't all be able to land with me — the seals scare easily. After I'm through, I'll join you for the picnic.' He chuckled. 'Can't beat being paid to enjoy yourself, can you?'

'Jammy beggar,' said Tony with a grin and clapped him on the shoulder. 'Let's go, Greg.'

We all filed down the steps, which near the bottom were semi-submerged, and slippery and treacherous with green weed. I clutched the rail and was glad of Greg's outstretched hand to help me over the gunwale and into the boat.

His grip was strong and warm and as I glanced up at him our eyes met. I felt a sudden lurch of . . . what? Something significant, certainly. Recognition on a deeper level? Mutual attraction? But that was out of the question — although I knew he held on to my hand a fraction longer than was absolutely necessary — for Phil was on my other side and now placed a firm hand around my waist as the boat rocked.

Greg had turned to help Lisa in the same way as, with a lot of giggling and clutching at his arm, she stumbled to a seat opposite me.

I wasn't sure about Lisa. Yesterday when we'd been playing with the ball I'd had the impression that she and Greg were a pair, and watching them closely now, I noticed how she played up to him all the time. As Greg took the wheel and prepared to cast off, Lisa slid along the seat until she was as near to him as she could get, looked archly up at him with some comment that was drowned by the roar of the engine, and swept back her long hair with a movement that could only be described as seductive. Greg cast her a brief distracted smile, but all his attention was on what he was doing.

I gave a mental shrug and turned my attention to the scenery as the boat pulled out of the harbour and headed out across the wide cornflower-blue sea.

It was thrilling, exhilarating and utterly beautiful. As the wind lifted my hair and took my breath away, I reached for Phil's hand to share the experience with him. He turned to me with a smile and a raised eyebrow, then gave my fingers a squeeze and let our joined hands lie passively on his knee.

I looked back over my shoulder. The

coastline was rapidly receding, reducing the towering cliffs and the jumbled roofs of cottages and caravans to toy-town size, and the hills beyond were becoming lost in a misty purple haze. Conversation was impossible over the roar of the engine, so I leaned back as the boat bucked and skipped over the waves and laughed with pure pleasure into the wind streaming past us.

After about half an hour I noticed that Greg was turning the boat in a curve towards the land, and soon I could see a rocky promontory with towering cliffs as a backdrop and several large caves gaping like open mouths at its foot. White water sucked and swirled inside the caves, and beyond there was a tiny shingle beach covered with rocks.

Greg cut the engine and we glided farther in on the tide.

'Here we are — Seal Cove,' he said, keeping the boat steady and its side clear with a long pole. 'This is as far as we go. Any farther in and we risk frightening them away.'

'You set, Tony?' He jerked his head and Tony scrambled out and on to the flat rocks, which shelved upwards in a series of natural steps, to take the rope which Greg tossed to him. He made it fast and jumped nimbly back into the boat again.

I shaded my eyes with a hand and looked expectantly round for the seals, but couldn't see any.

I turned to Janine with a frown. 'So where are they, all these seals?'

Her brown eyes widened as she lowered her binoculars and she pointed a finger.

'Over there, look — I've just counted thirty and there are some more in that cave.'

As the sun went behind a cloud I realised that some of the big blobs I had taken for rocks were, in fact, moving about.

'Oh!' I clapped a hand to my mouth, feeling foolish as Janine laughed.

'Here, take a look through these,' she

said, holding up her dark ponytail with one hand as she lifted the cord from around her neck and passed the binoculars to me.

'Thanks. I do feel silly,' I remarked as I took the glasses from her.

I turned to share the joke with Phil, but he had gone forward and was intent on angling his camera over the bow, so I raised the glasses and peered through the lenses.

The harder I looked the more seals I saw. Some were absolutely huge, obviously male, and varying in colour from black through all shades of grey to a rusty brown. So good was their camouflage that even with the binoculars I couldn't be certain which were in fact animals and which the rocks they were lazing around on.

Some were stretched out in the cove like sunbathers, others were rolling around in play or inching themselves slowly over the shingle either to or from the water.

'They're fantastic!' I exclaimed. 'I've

never seen anything like this. Absolutely amazing.'

'They are, aren't they?' Greg remarked over my shoulder, and I turned to him with a smile as he sat down in Phil's place. 'They look so awkward on land, but as soon as they enter the water they're transformed. You would never believe how agile they can be, and how fast.'

I glanced briefly at him, then, as I looked back through the lenses, I caught a distant movement and pointed a finger.

'There goes one now,' I said, as a small slate-coloured body slid effortlessly off a rock into the deep water beneath and headed out to sea. 'Oh, yes, wow, I see what you mean!'

I turned my attention back to what Greg was saying.

'The plan is, we stay here and watch the seals for a bit longer while John gets his stuff together and climbs in over the rocks to do what he has to do, then we'll go round the point and wait until he's ready to be picked up. There's a big sandy beach there.'

I nodded and handed the binoculars back to Janine with a grateful smile as Greg moved away to talk to John.

I noticed that Lisa had sidled up to Greg and caught hold of his arm as if to steady herself, although the boat was hardly moving.

'Are they a pair, Greg and Lisa?' I said in a low voice to Janine. She shrugged one shoulder and opened her hands, palms up in a 'search me' gesture.

'I'm sure Lisa would like to think so, but I'm not so sure about Greg. He doesn't seem to treat her any differently from the rest of us — it's Lisa who appears to do all the running. Mind you, Greg's never short of girls. I think he plays the field as he wants to.'

I nodded. That figured, I thought. With his looks, Greg would only have to raise a finger to have women queuing at his side in droves.

To my embarrassment he turned

around then, caught me watching him and grinned broadly. I felt colour flood my face and instantly looked away, making some trite remark to Phil at my side.

Then Greg called out, 'Hold on, everybody, we're leaving now,' and Tony pushed us off from the rocks and poled the boat a few yards out to sea before Greg started the engine and we headed round the promontory to the next cove.

This curved in a graceful arc of smooth firm sand, as golden as anything promised by the holiday brochures, and was completely deserted. After my initial surprise I could see why, for it was accessible only by sea or by a narrow, tortuous track, which threaded its wandering way down the sheer face of the cliff. It definitely wasn't a place to bring a family.

★　★　★

'Did you get some good shots of the seals?' I asked Phil, after we had helped to haul the boat out of the water and were tramping up the beach together towards the dry sand underneath the cliff.

'I'll say,' he replied with enthusiasm as he swung his camera off his shoulder and carefully replaced it in its carrying case. 'They were great, weren't they?'

Pleased to see him so happy, I nodded in agreement as we sat down and prepared to soak up the sunshine.

'We've got about an hour before I go back for John, then we'll eat our lunch,' Greg announced to the group in general. 'OK?'

'OK,' came the unanimous response as everybody settled down to do their own thing.

Janine and Tony had stripped for a swim and were already racing each other down the beach, which left Lisa, Greg, Phil and me.

Lisa stretched herself out on a towel, Phil had opened his photography book and Greg was watching the antics of the two in the sea, his forearms resting on his drawn-up knees. And I was watching him, for he intrigued me.

On the surface, he seemed to be everybody's friend, a handsome hunk with not a care in the world, never short of company both male and female, but I wondered. He never gave any of himself away, and in repose, as now, I noticed that his features had changed from those of the happy-go-lucky character he portrayed most of the time and were set in an expression of — what? Not worry, exactly; preoccupation, certainly. I had the impression that there was something on his mind that he wasn't sharing.

Hmm — mystery man.

I shrugged and turned away to dabble my hand in a small, round rock-pool fringed with ribbons and lace of pink and green weed, its crystal-clear water warm to the touch. Jelly-like blobs of sea anemones clung to the sides and I saw a tiny shining fish emerge from under a stone. Then, probably seeing my shadow looming over it, with a flick of its silver tail it was gone in an instant, diving under the weed for cover.

'Have you made any further progress with your research, Ginny?' Greg's voice broke into my thoughts and I jerked around, shaking the water from my fingers and wiping them on my jeans. The familiar open smile was back on his face and he seemed genuinely interested.

'Oh — no — no, I haven't,' I replied. 'Somehow I can't bring myself to tackle all those newspapers, especially in this lovely weather.' I shrugged. 'It was OK when it was raining, but I can't concentrate when the sun's shining outside!'

He chuckled, and laughter lines crinkled up the corners of his eyes.

'I know what you mean,' he said, then paused for a moment, before adding, 'There might be another road you could go down though.' Our eyes met.

'Oh? What's that?' I asked expectantly.

'How long ago is it that your mother

died?' he asked.

I could answer that one without having to think about it.

'Twenty-five years — soon after I was born,' I replied. 'Why?'

He had picked up a piece of driftwood and was absently scoring patterns in the sand at his feet.

'And how old was she then?'

I had to think for a moment.

'Um — she would have been thirty-three, the same age as my father,' I replied, wondering what all this was leading up to.

Greg scratched some figures in the sand with a stick, then, looking up, he remarked, 'So that would make her fifty-eight now, if she'd lived. Uh-huh.' He nodded.

'Yes, I suppose so,' I said. 'Why do you ask?'

Greg tossed away the stick and folded his arms as he gazed thoughtfully at me.

'Because if you know where she came from, I'm sure you would find people still living there who would have known her — don't you think so? Fifty-eight isn't that old, after all; it's not as if they'd have died off or become forgetful through being really elderly. And you could talk to them direct. You'd be more likely to find out personal stuff that way than from newspaper reports.'

'What a brilliant idea!' I felt my face light up with excitement. 'Why didn't I think of that myself?'

Greg shook his head, as he said, 'No, I should have been the one to think of it, and before now. In my line of work there's no excuse. But I wasn't thinking straight. I imagined that it had all happened much longer ago.'

He smiled broadly, I suppose because of my obvious delight.

'Yes — personal stuff,' I repeated, talking almost to myself as my mind turned the idea over. 'That's what I need to know. I need to find someone who actually knew her.'

'My grandmother was always making these snide remarks, you know?' I half turned towards Greg and he nodded. 'I used to listen behind closed doors when she had visitors and I heard her say things . . . Like how my father — apparently he was a gifted engineer — 'threw himself away on that woman, after all that disgraceful business too.' And, 'She made a perfect fool of him . . . ' That sort of thing.'

Greg's face was full of sympathy. 'How did the accident happen?' he asked. 'Or don't you know that either?'

'Oh, yes,' I replied. 'They were on their way down to Cornwall to visit her family. Apparently the weather was appalling and he'd never driven that way before. They were partway across the Goss Moor when the car skidded and crashed head-on with another vehicle. My parents died instantly. The people in the other car survived, fortunately — and by some miracle I survived, too. I can't remember a thing about it, of course.'

I glanced at Greg again. He had fallen silent and was gazing out to sea with such a look of sadness about him that I was intrigued. Surely the story of my long-dead parents wasn't *that* moving for him?

I was about to speak when he gave a sigh and remarked almost to himself, 'Yes, tragedies happen sometimes, at the most unexpected times.' Which reinforced what I had been thinking earlier. There was something of a darker nature behind this man's ready smile and laid-back manner.

At that moment a movement from Lisa distracted Greg from his train of thought, as she sat up.

'I need some sun-cream on my back,' she announced, rummaging in her bag and pulling out a yellow bottle. 'Greg, be a love and do my shoulders, will you?' she added, fixing me with a look that spoke volumes. It was clearly saying, 'Hands off — he's mine.'

I gave her my sweetest smile in return as Greg brushed the sand off his hands.

'Right,' I said as he turned away. 'Thanks for the tip. I'll certainly try to find some contacts. I know my mother came from St Agnes, and that's just along the coast from here,' I added, mostly to myself as Lisa thrust the yellow bottle into his hand.

'Did you hear all that, Phil?' I nudged him with an elbow.

'Um, not really,' he muttered, looking up from his book.

I sighed, and began to tell him the whole story.

So Jealous!

Shortly afterwards a bank of cloud blew over, forcing Lisa to abandon her sunbathing, and she and Greg strolled down the beach together to paddle along the edge of the water, deep in conversation, where they met up with the other two just emerging after their swim.

Soon after they had all arrived back in a bunch, I heard Greg's mobile phone ring.

'That was John,' he announced after he'd answered it. 'He's finished the job, so I'm going round to pick him up. Come and give me a hand, Tony, OK?'

Tony scrambled willingly to his feet. 'Sure, mate,' he replied and followed him down the beach.

'So, Phil,' I said, as I finished relating to him what Greg had suggested, 'shall we go to St Agnes tomorrow and start asking around?' I could hardly sit still from eagerness to put the new idea into practice. Then I caught sight of Phil's frown and darkening expression, so before he could speak I added quickly, 'It's a beautiful place, I believe. There are some old preserved mine workings there and the cliffs round about are supposed to be spectacular. I'm sure you'd find it very interesting. You could probably get some great atmospheric shots.'

But Phil was glowering at me with eyes which had become as hard and round as the pebbles on the beach.

'Oh no, Virginia,' he muttered, shaking his head, 'don't try to get round me like that. You ought to know by now that you can't fool me into thinking that you're going over there for my benefit. I know you too well.'

I sighed. That was just it — he did. We'd been together for so many years. How long was it now? I had to think for a minute. It must be four this summer — so long that we'd become almost like an old married couple, a pair who knew each other inside out and could anticipate what the other's reaction would be to any given situation before they'd even spoken.

A small shiver feathered down my spine as suddenly I heard a little enquiring voice pipe up inside my head: 'Well, Virginia Shaw, is this how you want it to be for the rest of your life?' it asked. 'Don't you think this relationship has become stale? Could it be that you're both taking each other for granted these days? And what happened to *romance?*' it hissed.

That little voice brought me up short and made me really focus on our relationship, forcing me to see it as it actually was. For months now I'd been trying to ignore the signs of strain that were there, not far below the surface, and turn a blind eye to the cracks that I was constantly pasting over to keep Phil in a good mood.

Now I thought rebelliously, Why should I have to? and sternly asked myself how much he really meant to me?

Then I had to admit sadly that, yes, he was a friend, a good friend — but *only* a friend. And I realised that I'd been letting things run on in the same old way for far too long, rather than rock the boat by having a confrontation, because I'd been afraid of what it would lead to. Coward! I told myself. You're doing no favours to either Phil or yourself, and it's time you brought matters to a head.

Huh — brave words! I glanced at Phil's mutinous expression and nibbled my bottom lip as I realised I would have to bide my time and wait for the right opportunity to present itself. If not, this would quite possibly develop into a flaming out-and-out row, where we might end up saying things that we would both regret later.

'Well, it's just something to think about,' I replied lightly, refusing to be drawn, and ready to put it all on temporary hold at the back of my mind.

But Phil obviously wasn't willing to let it go, and his temper flared as he jumped to his feet and snapped, 'It seems to me that the whole of our so-called 'holiday' has been geared to this obsession of yours!' His face flushed an angry brick red. 'I think I've been very patient so far, although I've hardly seen you for days on end. But now I'm telling you, Virginia, I've had enough of it. Here we are with only a couple of days left — you've found absolutely nothing that you didn't know before, and now you're talking about this latest hare-brained scheme which will occupy the short time we have left! You're being completely self-centred — selfish through and through.'

I glanced towards the others to see if they could hear, but they'd taken a ball farther down the beach and were kicking it around well out of earshot.

'And *you're* exaggerating the whole thing!' I retorted, biting my lip as I felt tears of frustration threatening to overwhelm me. However, with great determination I willed myself to stay in control, for if I dissolved now it would give him the perfect opening for saying, 'There, you see — I told you so — you've been overdoing it. I know you better than you know yourself.'

I could already imagine the smug look and the patronising pat on the back he would give me as he enveloped me in his arms, and I wondered sadly where it had all gone wrong, how had we lost the love and the trust there had been between us at the beginning?

I folded my arms and stared out to sea, instantly feeling a burden of guilt descend on my shoulders, then I wondered rebelliously why on earth he *should* be able to make me feel that way.

Phil turned away, still smouldering, and flopped down on the sand again.

Unable to keep still with my mind in such a jangle, I got up and walked away to stride restlessly up and down among the smaller rocks and poke about in the caves behind us, as I tried to calm my racing thoughts.

Moodily I decided that there was nothing to be gained from pursuing the argument for the moment, so on the way back to 'base' I temporarily swallowed my resentment as I tried to think of something to offer as an olive branch to the hunched figure who had now returned to his book.

Then, fortunately, out of the corner of my eye I caught sight of movement in the distance and seized upon it as a welcome diversion.

'Oh, look, here comes the boat,' I said brightly. 'We can have lunch now they're all back. I'm starving, how about you?'

Phil grunted and placed a marker in his book before laying it to one side. He always had a proper leather bookmark with him, however far away from home he travelled, and was never reduced to using a scrap of torn newspaper or an old train ticket as I would have been.

'Not exactly *starving* — and neither

are you,' he said pedantically. 'When you think of famine in Africa, that's starving. But I'm certainly peckish, yes. What have we got?'

I sat down and rummaged in one of the bag.

'Sandwiches, and plenty of them!' I said with a forced laugh. 'I think I've probably overdone it, but they all looked so tempting in the deli that I couldn't resist.'

I pulled out a plastic box and opened it.

'Cheese and pickle, egg and salad, ham and tomato, tuna and mayonnaise.' I rattled off the list and pushed the box towards Phil.

'Good grief, girl, there's enough here to feed an army!' he exclaimed, dipping a hand inside, and I gave a sigh of relief at the lightening of his mood.

By this time the others had all returned and had clustered in a group around us, eating and talking at the same time. Joining in the camaraderie and the friendly banter, I suddenly realised how much I was enjoying being in Cornwall, especially in this lovely spot, and felt a pang of disappointment at the thought that the holiday was almost over.

It was because I was feeling more at home here than I'd ever felt in Birmingham where I'd grown up, or in London where I'd trained and had been working for six years. Maybe the Cornish side of me, which had come down from my mother, was taking over and telling me that this was where I belonged. For that was what it felt like — belonging, as if the rest of my life so far had only been leading up to this point, to this place where I was *meant* to be.

I glanced at Phil, who was deep in conversation with John, apparently about photography, and wondered . . .

We were only going back because *his* fortnight's leave was up. But *I* had the whole of the school holidays — another month at least.

I nibbled my lip and bit deeply into a sandwich as my mind began to whirl.

If — and it was a big if — Phil would agree to go back *without* me, I could stay on for that time and take as long as I liked to follow up Greg's idea of talking to people.

The idea was so attractive that I felt a stab of guilt at feeling so pleased about it. Then I thought for the second time that day, why on earth *should* I feel guilty? We were both free individuals, for goodness' sake.

However, that didn't make it any easier to bring up the subject.

I would have to choose my time very carefully. In fact, we had a *lot* of talking to do.

A Surprising Discovery

'So how were the seals, John?' I asked. He was sitting not far away, munching crisps, with a preoccupied expression on his face and his eyes on the sea.

He started as I spoke and seemed to come back from a long way off.

'Oh, hi, Ginny! Um, not too good actually,' he replied, crumpling up the empty bag and stuffing it in his backpack. 'I found several sick ones, I'm afraid. They were easy to spot because they stayed on the beach while I approached, while those that were fit were off into the water when they saw me coming.'

'How sad!' I could understand now why he seemed so glum. 'So what did you do?'

John was unscrewing the top of his flask and I he poured some tea into the cap and took a swig before he replied.

'I tranquillised each one, counted them, and then phoned the seal sanctuary. They're on their way to pick them up and take them back for hospitalisation.'

'You mean there's a hospital for *seals*?' My voice rose in amazement and John looked surprised.

'Oh, yes. It's over at Gweek, on the other coast. Didn't you know?'

I shook my head. 'I've never heard of it,' I said.

'But then, she doesn't come from round here, John, remember.' Greg's voice joined in the conversation.

'No, I know that, but the sanctuary is quite famous,' John said. He turned to me and went on, 'We get a lot of injured seals washed up, mostly in the winter after a storm, but some get snagged in fishing lines as well. People contact the sanctuary if they find one. It's always a busy place.'

'I don't know a thing about seals, really.' I shrugged, hugging my knees and resting my chin on them. 'I've never come across any before.'

John smiled. 'It's time for a natural history lesson then,' he said. 'I'll get into full lecturing mode.' He jokily cleared his throat and struck a pose, then began, 'The females give birth to their pups in the autumn — '

'*Autumn?*' I echoed, interrupting him. 'That's a strange time to have young ones, isn't it?'

John nodded. 'They develop very rapidly,' he replied. 'They're mostly grown by now, as you saw. Very soon the whole colony will spend most of its time out at sea and then come back to the cove in autumn to breed again.'

'They're fascinating animals, aren't they?' said Greg. 'Those huge eyes always look so soulful — almost human. What did you say you Scots people call them, John? There was a name — I can't remember . . . '

'Oh, in Scotland they're known as silkies,' John replied with a grin. 'There's a lot of folklore around the islands about silkies.'

I raised a hand to shade my eyes as the sun shifted round.

'Such as?' I asked, squinting at him.

'Such as,' John said, 'that they are seals by day, but at nightfall they change out of their seal-coats and become human.'

I burst out laughing, but at the same time I found the notion quite charming.

'Like mermaids then,' I added, 'who leave the sea behind and creep up to the village at night. We went down to Zennor the other day, didn't we, Phil?' I said, trying to include him, and he gave a brief nod. 'There's a famous mermaid story there. I suppose you all know it.' I looked towards Greg.

'Oh, yes, of course,' he said, taking up the thread. 'So you've been in the church, obviously, and seen the bench-end carved with her image.'

I nodded. 'With a comb in one hand and a mirror in the other. But that mermaid went back to the sea, didn't she? And took her lover with her.'

'Maybe,' John went on, 'but a silkie,

so they say, if he or she happens to lose its coat, or has it stolen while it's away, can never return to the sea, and is doomed to stay in the world of humans for ever.' His voice dropped and fell silent, and his gaze shifted out to sea again as if he was hoping to see a gleam of golden hair or the flick of a fishy tail.

'I've read tales of fishermen,' Greg said into the silence, 'who have sworn they've seen mermaids when they're at sea, and heard them singing. I expect those must have been seals. Not that the noise they make could remotely be calling singing.' He chuckled. 'Have you heard it, Ginny?'

I shook my head.

'It's a deep, moaning kind of boom that echoes up the cliff and can give you goose pimples if you don't know what it is! A bit like this,' he added, making such a ghastly noise that we all fell about laughing, even Phil.

However, towards the end of the afternoon the cloud that had drifted over thickened and a cool breeze sprang up, so by common consent we began putting our things together and getting ready to leave. We were just moving down the beach towards the boat when the first few drops of rain fell.

'Ugh!' Janine said, looking up at the sky as we all piled into the boat. 'You'd think it could have held off for just another hour, wouldn't you?' She shrugged herself into a waterproof jacket as I zipped up my own and pulled the hood firmly over my head.

By the time Greg and Tony had pushed the boat the few yards into the water and jumped in themselves, it was pouring, and although we all huddled together as low as we could, there was no real protection from it.

'It looks like it's set to last, too,' I said, squeezing in between Janine and Lisa and pushing my cold hands up inside my sleeves.

As we rounded the protection of the point and headed out into the open sea, the wind strengthened and I glanced towards Phil who had, of course, against all advice, refused to bring any rainwear. His shirt and shorts were already sodden, and I could see that his teeth were chattering.

Greg had obviously noticed as well, for Phil was sitting as near the wheelhouse as he could get, trying to shelter, and Greg took one hand off the wheel and tossed him a piece of yellow tarpaulin.

'Here, mate,' he yelled over the noise of the engine, 'wrap that round you.'

I couldn't believe it when Phil shook his head and shouted back with false bravado, 'Oh, I'm OK. I'll give it to one of the girls.'

He made a great show of tossing it to Lisa, who sensibly took one corner and handed the other to Janine, so that they were able to form a kind of tent which was big enough to include me as well.

You silly idiot, I thought, staring at Phil in amazement. He caught my glance and immediately looked away with a thunderous expression on his face. Arms folded, he hunched in his seat, looking such a picture of misery that I had to stifle a smile. He had brought it all on himself through trying to be some kind of macho man, and I couldn't summon up much sympathy for him.

I was thinking, though, that obviously tonight would not be the right time to suggest that I'd like to stay on here without him. I'd planned to tell him when we got back, but now I would have to wait for a more appropriate moment.

*   *   *

Tactfully I decided not to mention going to St Agnes again, and neither did Phil. We spent the next day, the last one of our holiday, touring around the magnificent coastline and finishing up at Land's End.

It had been a companionable kind of day. The summer weather had returned in all its glory as if apologising for yesterday's downpour, and Phil was over the moon at some fantastic shots he had taken, so as we sat outside a café indulging ourselves with a cream tea, I decided that the moment had come. After all, I could hardly leave it any longer, though it did seem a shame to ruin the moment.

So, having waited until we'd nearly finished so as not to spoil the meal, I took a deep breath and said, 'Phil, there's something I want to talk to you about.'

He licked a blob of jam off his thumb and wiped it in his napkin.

'Mm?' He raised enquiring eyes to my face.

I took another breath and opened my mouth, realising that I was actually shaking with nerves, and hated myself for being like this. Surely, I thought rebelliously, partners in a good relationship should be able to say anything to each other without having to take out every word and look at it before speaking, shouldn't they? So what did that say about us?

At last I plunged in and Phil listened intently, his eyes never leaving my face until I stuttered to a close and silence fell.

I fixed my attention on the spectacular colours with which the sun was painting the western sky as it wheeled its way towards the horizon, throwing the distant finger of the Longships Lighthouse into stark relief.

His reaction was bad, worse even than I had anticipated. All through the journey back and that evening, his attitude swung from towering rage to icy, tight-lipped silence or hurt and wounded self-righteousness.

During all this I felt like some small beleaguered creature that had retreated into its shell for protection, and I kept my head down and my own temper under wraps, determined not to give him the satisfaction of an out-and-out row. I was staying on, and that was that.

We both knew — for I'm sure that Phil was aware of it, too, without putting it into words — that this row was about more than just the holiday. This was the big one, where we would part company for good.

The next morning, hatchet-faced, Phil appeared with his bag packed and I drove him to the station.

However, as he stepped on to the train and I noticed the hurt behind the fury in his face, I almost put out a hand to say how sorry I was it had ended like this and that we could still be friends, couldn't we? But a glance at his forbidding expression stopped the words in my throat and we parted with a strained and brief, 'Goodbye.'

As I drove back, I found my hands on the wheel trembling in the aftermath of all this, and my throat was tight with unshed tears.

Four years was a long time and I was going to miss him. We'd had some really good times in the past, but they were in the past and now I had to look to the future — a future on my own, which to begin with would seem very strange.

By the time I arrived back, however, my spirits had begun to lift and I had to admit that my overall feeling was one of relief more than anything else. The break had been made and now the rest of the holidays were mine to do what I liked with.

To my delight, the cottage was free for the following fortnight at least, due to a cancellation, so I wouldn't have to move out.

I made myself a strong coffee, put my feet up and gazed out over the bay. Even the sparkling sea seemed to be reflecting the smile I knew was spread all over my face, for this afternoon I would go and explore St Agnes.

★　★　★

What I found was a small but busy town with a picturesque cove, and with relics of its mining past looming everywhere in the shape of tall chimneys and man-made caves burrowed deep into its spectacular cliffs.

It was all very diverting, but I was here for a purpose. But quite where was I to start? I had no idea.

I parked the car and leaned on the steering wheel, wondering, and as I did so my attention was drawn to the parish church nearby. Inside the porch I could see a notice board. I might as well have a quick look at that and see what was going on in the place.

There was the flower rota for the next month. Meetings of the junior church, an approaching summer fete, and the forthcoming programme for the Over Fifties' Club, which was held on Friday afternoons in the church hall.

That instantly sparked an idea in my head. Old people! Well — oldish, anyway. And today was Friday — how was that for a coincidence?

I glanced at the programme again. According to this they should be having a talk about health and fitness.

I crossed the road and found the church hall. Peals of laughter, the clatter of crockery and a buzz of chatter met me as I pushed open the door. It was obviously teatime, so presumably the talk was over.

Just inside the door was a table where a woman who seemed to be presiding over the meeting was poring over a large ledger spread open in front of her and drinking tea as she ran a finger down a column of names, while the body of the hall was filled with groups of people, mainly women, sitting around on rows of plastic chairs.

'Can I help you?' The woman glanced up as she noticed me. 'Are you looking for someone?'

I smiled, as the question was so apt.

'Yes,' I replied, 'I am, but I'm going to need a great deal of help to find her.'

The woman's brows rose as I slipped into a chair beside her and explained what I was after. Then as she began to understand, she gave a chuckle.

'Oh, I see,' she said, and nodded. 'Well, now.' She held out a hand. 'I'm Jennifer Leigh, and you are . . . ?'

I told her and shook the proffered

hand. In her sixties, I thought, grey hair swept up in a chignon, slender and smartly dressed, with a kindly face and lively hazel eyes.

She listened closely while I told her my mother's name and the relevant dates I knew of, but when I came to the end she shook her head and said, 'I'm afraid I can't help you, my dear. I only came down here to live after my husband retired a few years ago.'

Disappointment hit me with a thud — but what had I expected? That the first person I met would turn out to have been my mother's best friend or something? Get real, I told myself. Coincidences like that just don't happen.

But as I looked around at all the grey heads in the room I thought, surely *some* of these people must be local? However, Jennifer was saying something else as she looked around the room.

'Most of the people here did the same,' she remarked. 'Come down here to retire, I mean. We do get local people but I don't think there's anyone here today. This lovely weather has meant a small attendance — they're either away on holiday, or they've gone to the beach to enjoy it, or stayed in the garden . . . '

Her gaze swept the room, then she shook her head and turned towards me with a shrug.

I swallowed my disappointment and was preparing to leave when Jennifer put a hand on my arm and added, 'However, I have a sister, Rosemary, who has lived around here all her life, and she's fifty-eight, the same age as you say your mother would be now. You could ask her if you wanted to.'

My spirits shot back up again. 'Oh, yes! Yes, please!' I said eagerly.

Jennifer picked up a pen and wrote on a scrap of paper.

'There's her name and address. She doesn't go out a lot, her health isn't good, so I expect she'll be pleased to have a visitor, especially one who's interested in old times.' She smiled and added, 'I could phone her right away, if you like, and you could save yourself another journey.'

I took the paper as she pulled out a mobile phone and contacted her sister. The call was brief, and she nodded to me as she replaced the phone in her handbag.

'She's at home — I told her you'd be right over.'

I thanked her fervently, made my farewells, and left as the meeting was breaking up. I was walking on air as I went back to the car. I'd only been here for half an hour. It had been that easy!

On The Right Track

Rosemary Harris turned out to be a dumpy, motherly woman who answered the door to me leaning on a stick. The resemblance to her sister was there, but Rosemary's face was bare of make-up, more tanned, and her pale blue eyes regarded me from behind a pair of tinted glasses.

'You must be Virginia,' she said with a welcoming smile as she widened the door, and I nodded, smiling back at her.

'Ginny, please,' I said.

'Ah, right, Ginny. Jennifer phoned to say that you would be calling. Come in, my dear, come in.'

She led the way down a passage towards the back of the cottage.

It was set in the middle of a Victorian terrace, and through the window of the built-on conservatory where she led me, I could see a beautifully tended garden full of all the flowers of summer. Beyond it, a small stream threaded its way to the sea beneath leafy ranks of mature trees.

'Oh, how lovely!' I said as we settled ourselves in the comfortably padded cane furniture.

Rosemary smiled and nodded.

'Gardening's my passion,' she said simply, and added, 'since my husband died two years ago, it's been my lifeline as well.' She smoothed down the pleats of her navy linen skirt.

'Now,' she said in a business-like way, 'Jennifer said that you wanted to talk about the past. That you're trying to trace somebody. So, how can I help you?'

I opened my mouth to speak, then suddenly was tongue-tied with excitement, for I had just noticed that at the neck of her crisp white blouse Rosemary was wearing a brooch exactly like the one I carried everywhere with me, bearing the logo of the long-defunct

Chenoweth's foundry.

I rummaged in my bag and held it out to her.

'Look,' I said eagerly, 'this belonged to my mother. I'm trying to find out about her early life, when she lived down here. I can see that this is exactly like the one you're wearing, and as she would be your age now, I think you must have worked at Chenoweth's at the same time as she did. Her name was Caroline Rowe — they called her Carrie,' I finished a trifle breathlessly.

Rosemary shot up straight in her chair.

'You're Carrie's daughter?' she exclaimed. 'Well, bless my soul!'

She looked me closely up and down, then nodded.

'Yes, you do have a look of her about you. The Rowes were all blond and blue-eyed, with that distinctive pointed chin just like yours. Well, well, who'd have thought it, after all these years!'

'You knew her well, then, did you? And the family?' My heart was beating furiously as I willed her to get on with it and tell me everything, anything, any slightest bit of information that would help me form a picture of my shadowy mother.

'We were at school together,' Rosemary replied, 'although we were never exactly best friends, if you know what I mean. We both went straight from school into Chenoweth's, Carrie because her parents needed the money, and me because I was never much of a scholar — I was always better at practical things.'

I leaned forward eagerly.

'What was she like, Rosemary? I don't mean in looks, but what sort of a person was she?'

To my surprise a guarded expression came over the woman's face then, and she looked away from my direct gaze, her eyes on the bright flowerbeds outside the window, her fingers twisting in her lap.

Then she turned her attention back to me and replied, as if she had been choosing her words with care, 'On the quiet side, Carrie was. Friendly enough, but kept herself to herself, you know?'

I nodded. 'Go on,' I encouraged her.

'Oh, dear. It was rather a long time ago,' Rosemary replied, biting her lip. She was absently twiddling her wedding ring round and round on her finger, I noticed, and I had the distinct impression that there might be something she was keeping from me.

'Yes . . . and . . . ?' I pressed.

'They were all like that, the family. Proud. But hardworking, you know? They weren't very well off, there being so many of them, but the girls were always decently turned out when they came to school. And after they grew up and left home, things were easier. Carrie, being the youngest, had the best of it, really.'

'What happened to all the sisters?' I asked. 'I don't suppose you know where any of them are now?'

To my disappointment Rosemary shook her head.

'Sorry, dear, I've no idea. I lost touch with Carrie when I left the firm to get married. She worked on for several more years, I believe, before — ' She stopped abruptly, before hastily saying, 'So there we are,' as if winding up the conversation. But I wasn't going to let it end there.

'Before what?' I persisted, and she spread her hands in a look of defeat and sighed.

'I suppose you'll have to know, dear. Sooner or later you'll be bound to find out, and it might as well come from me as from anyone, I suppose,' she said, regarding me with something like pity.

My stomach lurched as I wondered whatever was coming.

'Yes?' I whispered, holding her gaze as her eyes met mine.

'I'm afraid, my dear, that your mother was found guilty of committing a crime, and spent six months in prison.'

I felt as if I'd been punched in the stomach. For a moment I felt sick as the room whirled around me and I struggled to take this in.

So that was it. Now I knew and understood why my grandmother had been so cold about her daughter-in-law, particularly as she had been so concerned all her life with appearances and 'what people will think.'

I loved her dearly but even I could see how strait-laced she was, how moralistic, and how completely unforgiving she would have been when faced with the shame of this happening in her own family. It was something that had never occurred to me in even my most fanciful dreams.

I moistened my dry mouth.

'*Prison?*' It came out as a croak and I had to clear my throat before adding, 'Wh — what did she do?'

Rosemary took a deep breath and gazed out over the garden again.

'Well, Carrie worked at Chenoweth's much longer than I did, as I said. I'd left to get married before it all happened, but I heard it all from someone who was still there.' She tapped her fingers on the arm of her chair and turned her attention back to me as she took a deep breath.

'Well, we both started on the shop floor after we left school, as I said, but Carrie was bright and ambitious and after a few years she applied for and was given a job in the accounts department, in the wages office.'

'I see.' I nodded, my gaze never leaving her face. 'And ... ?' I prompted.

Rosemary looked away again.

'Soon after that,' she muttered, 'a sum of money went missing from the safe. And only two people knew the combination number of it. One was the boss, the other was your mother.'

Her mouth closed in a hard line and an uncomfortable silence fell. My heart felt like a lead weight in my chest and I was finding it hard to breathe.

'I see,' I said again in a small voice, then added, 'Did she own up to it?'

Rosemary shook her head.

'Never. She swore that she was innocent, even after she'd been sentenced and served her term. Of course no one believed her. Everyone knew that she came from a poor family and assumed that the temptation had been too much for her, especially as she'd recently bought an expensive new winter coat, although she swore she'd saved up for it. And the money was never found.'

'Do you think she did it?' I asked as our eyes met.

'I don't honestly know what to think, even after all these years,' Rosemary replied. 'I just could never make up my mind. I know she had one good friend who stood by her all the time and never believed she was guilty — she even went into the witness box to speak up for her — but the fact remains,' she finished defiantly, 'that if Carrie didn't take the money, then who did?'

'Is this friend still around?' I said urgently. 'I'd love to speak to her as well.'

Rosemary nodded. 'Oh, yes, Sybil's around still. Sybil Trenwith, her name is — she lives just down the road. You can see her house from here.'

She stood up and went to the window where I eagerly followed her pointing finger.

'I'll go and see her,' I said, nodding and full of purpose again. 'Is it all right if I mention your name?'

Rosemary gave a broad smile — with relief that the conversation was over, I guessed.

'Oh, yes, yes, of course, dear,' she said as she led the way to the door to see me out. Probably she was glad to be rid of me and my questions.

But what a lot I'd learned from her in a short space of time. And what a revelation it had been. I felt mentally exhausted. But not too exhausted to walk down to the bungalow Rosemary had pointed out, hoping against hope that my next lead would be at home as well . . .

★ ★ ★

A young man in shorts and a vest was mowing the lawn as I arrived, and I hesitated outside the gate until he noticed me and turned off the motor.

'Can I help you?' he enquired as he took a few steps towards me. 'Are you lost?'

I shook my head. 'No, I'm looking for Mrs Trenwith,' I replied. 'I believe she lives here? Mrs Harris sent me.'

'Oh — Rosemary, yeah.' He jerked a thumb. 'Mum's up in the greenhouse, round the back. You'd best go round.'

I thanked him and followed the direction of the thumb, up a couple of granite steps round the side of the house, and along the path to the greenhouse where I could see a figure with her back to me, tying up tomato plants.

Not wanting to make her jump, I cleared my throat loudly, then tapped at the open door.

'Mrs Trenwith?' I said as she turned round and looked blankly at me. 'Hello. Your son said I might come round here and find you.'

'Yes?' Her brows rose enquiringly, and she rubbed her hands down the front of her print apron as she regarded me with interest.

I told her my name and repeated the story of my search into the past, mentioning Rosemary's name again along the way.

As lean and wiry as her friend was plump, she regarded me from clear blue eyes the colour of the sea behind her.

'So you're Carrie's daughter? Oh, my word!'

After her reaction, so similar to Rosemary's, she paused to take in this information, then said briskly, 'Well, you'd better come inside and I'll make a cup of tea — ' She picked up a ball of string from the floor and began to wind it up.

'Oh, I don't want to interrupt your work,' I said hastily. 'I could come back another time.'

But she shook her head and smiled.

'That's all right, my handsome,' she replied in a broad Cornish voice. 'I do always have a cuppa about now, and if I don't make one for Tim soon he'll be round asking me if the kettle have broken down!' She chuckled and a pair of dimples appeared in her rosy cheeks.

So we sat companionably on the patio while she poured our tea into dainty china cups and saucers, after handing Tim a large mug, which he took back with a cheery wave to where he was working.

I told my story again and added what Rosemary had told me — that Sybil had always believed in my mother's innocence regarding the theft.

'Of course I did, and shall do to my dying day,' she said stoutly. 'The soul of honesty, Carrie were. She wouldn't no more take money that didn't belong to her than she would fly. They said all sorts of things at the trial, mind you, about her family being poor and all that, but that weren't right, because her sisters had left home by then and they was earning their own money.' She nodded and compressed her lips into a thin line.

'Then they said, too, that Carrie was saving up for her bottom drawer. Well, all girls did in those days and it didn't mean nothing. And then the fact that she'd just bought a new coat was cited as 'proof'. But I knew she'd been saving for ages for that coat, bit by bit over months, because she told me so.'

Sybil took a mouthful of tea and frowned as she went on.

'I know for sure they only said she done it because they couldn't find no one else to point the finger at. There was never no shred of evidence, and they couldn't properly prove a thing. Made a scapegoat of her, they did. And I said so in the witness box.'

She wagged a finger and her brows rose with indignation.

'But it didn't make no scrap of difference. Poor Carrie.' Sybil's mouth drooped and there was a sudden dampness in her eyes.

'So what do you think happened,

Sybil?' I asked, on the edge of my seat. 'Could someone else have known the number of the safe?'

She wiped her eyes and pushed her handkerchief up her sleeve.

'Well,' she said with a sigh, 'there used to be this window cleaner came around. Called Reg, he was — shifty-looking character, never could stand him myself, but he used to flirt with the other girls. Thought he was God's gift, he did — and they thought he was wonderful, too. Always ogling us, he was, and sucking up to the bosses as well.' She pulled a face which showed she hadn't thought much of him.

'Anyway,' she went on, 'he would be up his ladder, see, and he could look straight into the office while he was working. I always thought he would have had a pretty good view of the safe from there, and he used to come round regular, too. Well, I think he could well have seen Carrie or the boss turning the combination and memorised it.'

'Quite friendly with the workmen,

too, Reg was. Used to come in and eat his pasty with them, lunchtimes and all. And I've always said there was nothing to stop him sneaking into the office in the lunch-hour when everyone was out.'

'That's where *I* do think the money went. But I couldn't prove nothing and nobody wouldn't listen to me, they was all so intent on accusing poor Carrie.' Her shoulders lifted on a sigh. 'She lost her job, of course, needless to say.'

I nodded and nibbled my bottom lip in thought.

'I suppose she must have met my father soon after she came out of prison,' I said almost to myself, and we fell silent while I turned over the whole story in my head.

Then, without much hope, but deciding it was worth a chance, I asked Sybil if she knew of any of my relations still living in the area.

'Um . . . ' She thought for a moment, her brow furrowed and her gaze following the flight of a honey-bee among a lavender bush nearby. Then her face suddenly cleared and she turned back to me.

'Ah-h! There's Ruby Williams over to Hayle — she was one of Carrie's cousins, I do believe. A first cousin, she would be.' Sybil's head was nodding away. 'Her mother was the eldest of the sisters — '

' — and Carrie was the youngest,' I finished, beaming at her.

So I *did* have a relation, and at this news my spirits soared again, no matter how distant she might be. Second cousin, something like that? But a relation nevertheless.

I left Sybil Trenwith with many thanks for her help and made my way back to the car in high excitement. Tomorrow I would go to Hayle and continue my quest, but for today I had quite enough to think about.

An Invitation

Hayle was a long sprawl of a town draped along the road to Penzance. Situated at the head of a tidal river it was, the guidebooks said, a port with a great industrial history, but with little left to show for it.

I enquired at the post office for Ruby Williams' address, thinking it the obvious place to begin. In the way of small towns, probably everybody knew everyone else, or was related to them.

So it turned out, and I was directed to the end house in a row of terraced cottages not far from the beach.

A ginger cat was sunning itself on the wall and comically turned over on its back with all four paws in the air when I spoke to it. I gave it a quick stroke then seized the brass knocker and banged on the door.

It was opened by an elderly woman

as tiny and small-boned as a bird, leaning on a stick. Her bright black eyes were also birdlike, and she regarded me quizzically as I asked her if she could spare a few minutes of her time, explaining that I was trying to trace someone from the past.

'We-ell, I don't know . . . ' she replied with a slight frown, and I realised that, in the way of old people, she was wary of the unexpected, in case it led to something she couldn't cope with. I could see her searching her mind for an excuse to get rid of me and my heart sank.

'I'm sorry,' she said at last, 'but my nephew's here at the moment and I don't see him very often, you see . . . '

'Oh, don't worry,' I replied and swallowed my disappointment. 'Another day, perhaps?'

She nodded and was about to withdraw, when a man's voice came booming down the hall.

'I've finished cutting the grass, Aunt Ruby — is there anything else?' he said, as he came nearer and looked over her shoulder. 'Oh, sorry — I didn't know you had a visitor.'

My stomach turned a somersault as our eyes met.

'*Ginny!*'

'*Greg!*'

We both exclaimed together, then burst out laughing.

'You two know each other?' said Ruby in bewilderment, looking at each of us in turn. 'Well, I never . . . You'd better come in after all, my dear.'

'Ginny, what are you *doing* here?' Greg asked, as we followed Ruby into her sitting-room and sat down.

'Oh, it's such a long story,' I said, 'but I found out that Mrs Williams is related to my mother.'

Greg's eyes widened and he opened his mouth to speak just as the old lady said, 'Call me Ruby, dear, everybody does.'

Putting aside her stick she eased herself into an armchair and leaned back against the cushions, and I explained in more detail why I had come to see her.

'So you're Carrie's daughter, dear? Well, well,' she said as I came to the end of my story. 'Yes, you do have a look of her about you. All the Rowe girls had that sharp chin and turned-up nose.'

I smiled and felt warmed by the remark, as if it somehow brought me closer to my mother.

Then the old lady gave me a shrewd look.

'How much do you know about your mother, Ginny?' she asked quietly, her eyes meeting mine.

'I know of her — um — disgrace,' I replied, as I looked down at my lap and twisted my hands together. 'That she was accused of stealing from her employers, and went to prison for it?'

I cast a sideways glance at Greg to see his reaction, but he was looking fixedly at his aunt and his face gave nothing away.

Ruby nodded. 'I didn't know much about it at the time,' she replied. 'We lived away for many years when my husband was alive, and I think my mother hushed it all up in her letters because of the shame — you know?'

I nodded. I knew, all right. I'd spent my young life in the shadow of that shame.

'But I heard rumours,' Ruby said, 'and put two and two together. Then just before she died, my mother told me the full story.'

'For years I've been wanting so much to find out about my mother's background,' I said softly, 'because my grandmother would never talk about her either. But I never expected to unearth anything like this.' To my horror I heard the break in my voice as emotion threatened to overcome me, and I felt my lips quiver.

Then I jumped like a nervous kitten as I felt a warm hand grasp mine and give it a comforting squeeze. When I raised misty eyes to Greg's face and saw the sympathy there, it was almost too much, but I sniffed and swallowed and the moment passed, although the warmth of his touch remained long after he had withdrawn his hand.

'I can understand your grandmother's feelings,' Greg remarked, 'but she must have known you would find out eventually.'

I nodded. 'I think she just hoped it wouldn't be in her lifetime,' I replied.

Then a thought occurred to me. In fact, it hit me with the force of a sledgehammer, and I'm sure the shock must have shown on my face as I looked at each of them in turn.

'Oh, my goodness!' I exclaimed. 'I've just thought of something! Greg, if you're Ruby's nephew, and she's my second cousin or something — then you and I must be related!'

Greg's eyes widened and he looked wonderingly back at me, obviously as surprised as I was. Then he slowly shook his head as if trying to work it out.

'No-o, that can't be right.' He frowned and Ruby broke in.

'No, it isn't,' she said, 'because Greg is my late husband's nephew, you see. We were never blessed with children of our own, unfortunately.' Her mouth drooped. 'I should have liked to have had a family, but . . . ' she shrugged and spread her hands ' . . . it just didn't happen.'

The smile was back on her face as she nudged Greg with an elbow and added, 'All I've got is this great good-for-nothing lump!'

Greg raised a playful fist at her and laughed, showing even white teeth in his tanned face. They were obviously very fond of each other.

'Go on, Aunt Ruby,' he teased, 'you know I'm really your favourite nephew.'

She gave a snort of laughter and patted my arm as she retorted, 'He knows he can say that safely enough — because he's my *only* nephew!'

Some time later, after several cups of tea and a lot of childhood reminiscences from Ruby, which filled in some of the gaps in my mother's life for me,

Greg and I left together. The old lady was looking very tired by now, but she made me promise I would come for another visit before I went back, and I told her truthfully that I would love to.

*　*　*

Greg strolled up the street with me to where I'd left the car, and as I searched for my keys I asked him where his own car was.

'Oh,' he replied, 'I live within walking distance — just up the hill there.' He jerked a thumb.

'You live in Hayle?' I replied, surprised, then shrugged. 'I don't know why I assumed you lived in Redruth — because you work there, I suppose.'

'My parents do,' Greg replied, 'but I wanted a place of my own, nearer the sea, for the surfing. I moved out after . . . ' his face darkened ' . . . well, a few years ago.' I paused expectantly but he didn't elaborate, so I opened the car door and slipped inside.

Just as I was closing it behind me, however, Greg put his hand on the frame and said casually, 'By the way, Ginny, the surf club's holding a beach barbecue and fancy dress party on Saturday night. I was wondering — since you're on your own now, would you like to come?'

I looked up into those entrancing blue eyes, at that irresistible smile, and my heart skipped a beat. Maybe Lisa's antenna had picked up on something I hadn't even known myself until now, as I felt a surge of powerful attraction towards this enigmatic man who seemed to keep his thoughts and feelings so firmly under wraps.

'Fancy dress? Oh, I don't know, Greg . . . ' I hesitated.

But, a party! My spirits lifted at the thought of a bit of fun. I had been occupied with the serious stuff for so much of this trip that it had hardly seemed like a holiday at all. It would be good to have something light-hearted to think about to stop me dwelling on my mother's disgrace. For, innocent or not, her story had left a shadow of disappointment on my mind which I found difficult to shake off.

'Oh, it'll be nothing elaborate,' Greg added, probably thinking that was the reason for my hesitation. 'No hired costumes or anything like that, I mean, so don't worry. And there certainly won't be any prizes either. The rules are that we just throw on anything we can find, the funnier the better.'

'Oh, I see. OK.' I said, smiling broadly, 'I'd love to come, Greg, thanks. I'll look forward to it.'

'We're having the barbie about seven, then going back to change and meeting up again for the party. Bring something to cook,' he added, closing the car door and standing back as I started the engine.

'Right — see you then,' he called and waved a hand as I drove off.

★　★　★

I spent the next few days racking my brains as to what to wear to the party. I only had what I'd packed to come on holiday so my choice was pretty limited.

At last, however, I settled on a brightly-coloured tiered skirt and a scoop-necked blouse. With a scarf tied kerchief-like round my head and some hoop earrings in my ears, I might pass as a fortune teller.

There was a small fringed tablecloth in the living-room, too — I could throw that around my shoulders for a shawl.

There . . . I examined myself critically in the mirror once I'd put it all together and nodded with satisfaction. Not bad for an improvised outfit!

I hung it carefully on the back of the door until Saturday.

'I See Danger . . .'

I caught a whiff of the barbecue long before I saw it, as I was crossing the beach, and followed the tantalising smell of cooking round a headland to a secluded spot where a few of the group were already gathered outside a large cave. I could see the rest of them out surfing, riding the waves with a grace and expertise that I envied.

Clad in wet suits, their black heads bobbing in and out of the water, they reminded me of the colony of seals we had gone out to see, and I wondered how the animals were faring. I hadn't heard any more about their sickness, so maybe it had all blown over.

There was a neatly-built fire pit in a sandy arc where the cave sheltered it from the wind, and on the grill above it Tony was turning burgers. He looked up with a smile as I approached, and I handed over my package of sausages.

'Hi, Ginny,' he said. 'I hope you're good and hungry — there's masses of food here!'

'I'm starving!' I replied, and suddenly an image of Phil popped into my mind. The last time I'd said that he'd told me off. I'd hardly thought about him since he'd gone and I felt a twinge of guilt. But I did miss him. Or, to be more correct, I missed having a partner . . .

It wasn't that I regretted splitting up with Phil, for it obviously hadn't been working out and never would have, but it was such a long time since I'd been on my own that it felt strange. I would sometimes be reading an article in the newspaper or a magazine, and look up with some remark about it on the tip of my tongue, ready to share, and, of course, there was no one to listen.

But, I told myself, once the holiday was over and I returned to my own home and my friends, the school routine would swallow me up again and I would be too busy to dwell on it.

Meanwhile, I was fortunate to have the company of this friendly bunch of people, and grateful to them for making me so welcome.

'Is there anything I can do to help?' I asked, but Tony shook his head.

'This is men's work,' he said, and waved me away with his fork.

'Over here, Ginny,' Janine called, and I joined the others at the entrance to the cave where a pile of paper plates and some bottles of drinks were laid out on a flat shelf of rock.

'This cave will be handy if it comes to rain,' I said, seating myself on the warm sand.

'Good organisation, eh?' she replied. 'We know how to look after ourselves.'

I smiled. 'Bet it's not the first time you've done this,' I said, looking out of the corner of my eye for Greg, but there was no sign of him, or Lisa either. They must be among the group of surfers who were now leaving the water, carrying their boards and shaking off their hoods.

'Get a move on!' Tony called out as they came nearer. 'Food's nearly ready.'

They waved in acknowledgement and began to run up the beach.

'Help yourself to drinks,' somebody else called out, 'and hold your plates out.'

At that moment Greg and Lisa arrived together, holding hands, and flopped down beside me.

'Just in time!' Greg said with a smile, shaking himself like a dog. 'I shan't bother to change, the sun'll soon dry us out. Food's more important!'

Tony approached with a tray of food and I helped myself as Greg reached for a plate and piled it high, then stretched out his long legs and leaned back against the rock with a grunt of satisfaction.

'Ah, this is the life,' he remarked, taking a huge bite of his burger, then he added with a sigh, 'and to think that next week I shall be back at work.'

Lisa had seated herself on his other side and was toying with a chicken leg.

'Never mind.' She patted his arm consolingly. 'You'll still have the evenings. It won't be dark until late. We can come down again then.'

So, I thought with a pang, it seems to be 'we' after all with those two, whatever Janine might say.

There were beach games after the meal, but not for long as we all had to get home to change for the party, so quite soon we all pitched in on the clearing up.

I was standing at the entrance to the cave, scraping leftovers into a carrier bag and stacking the empty plates, when I became aware of a murmur of voices from inside. I couldn't help overhearing, although when I realised it was Greg and Lisa in there, I tried to move away. The last thing I wanted to do was to eavesdrop on them, but I was in the middle of my job and couldn't very well abandon it. So I stayed where I was.

It sounded as if they were having an argument. I picked up Lisa saying,

' . . . after all we've been to each
other . . . ' in an accusing tone, and,
' . . . and the way I supported you after
the accident, you know I did. And
now . . . '

'You did,' came Greg's deep rumble
as he replied, 'and I was grateful
because I needed all the support I
could get then, and you were a good
friend . . . '

Lisa said something else that I didn't
catch, then it was Greg again: 'But,
Lisa, that doesn't mean that I feel for
you anything more than friendship. I'm
sorry if you thought otherwise, but
there we are . . . '

'It's funny that it's only since *she*
came on the scene that you've started
feeling like that.' Lisa's tone had
changed to a venomous hiss. 'And don't
try to deny it. I've seen her making eyes
at you, and you bending over backwards to help with her so-important
'*research*'.'

I felt my eyes pop with amazement.
This was *me* she was talking about?

'So important,' she was going on, 'that you even have to go over it in your spare time when you're on the beach!'

Greg's indignant reply followed in such a low tone that I missed it. Then came the sound of footsteps crunching on shingle as if they were coming towards the entrance. I hastily gathered up the last of the rubbish and hurried down the beach to join the others.

By the time the two emerged with faces like thunder I was piling sand on the embers of the fire.

I was astounded at what I'd over-heard and my mind raced as I took it all in. So Lisa was jealous? Of me? The whole idea was laughable. Although I couldn't deny that I did feel attracted to him, the plain truth was that Greg had never said or done the slightest thing to indicate that he felt the same way about me.

And he had told Lisa straight out that they were only friends! So Janine had been right after all. I felt my mouth curve up at the corners and hummed a little tune as I smoothed over the patch where the fire had been and obliterated all signs of if.

* * *

Later that evening I was irritated to find my stomach full of butterflies as I crossed the beach and made my way up to the surfers' headquarters. But what was there to be nervous about, for goodness sake, I scolded myself — it's only a party.

But was my costume good enough? Did I look silly with a tablecloth round my shoulders? I'd had nobody to ask what they thought of my outfit, and was feeling very alone again.

I swallowed on a dry throat as I left the beach and crossed the strip of concrete up to the building.

Loud music was blaring out as I approached, and I could also hear the clink of glasses and occasional bursts of laughter from the upper storey, where several people were leaning on the railings of the balcony which ran around it.

I slipped in, edging my way around a stack of yellow canoes and some surfboards, which were overflowing from the understairs space where they had been stowed, climbed the stone steps, and paused on the threshold of the upper room.

The lighting was low, the disco beat was throbbing and some people were already out in the middle of the room dancing to it. I stood for a moment as my eyes adjusted to the light and I took in the motley assortment of costumes.

There were lots of people I didn't know, of course, but I picked out Janine's small, round figure standing at the side of the room in front of the drinks table, and edged my way round towards her. As I drew nearer I could see she was talking to a clown whom I realised was Tony. Janine was dressed as a doll in a short frilly dress, with white socks, rouged rosy cheeks and a huge bow in her hair, and she raised a hand as she saw me coming.

'Hi, Ginny! Glad you could come,' she greeted me with a smile. 'You look terrific!' she added, her round eyes raking me up and down.

'So do you two,' I replied, returning the compliment as I helped myself to a drink. 'So does everybody, actually,' I added, looking around. 'It's amazing what you can do with a bit of imagination.'

As pirates and gladiators, nursery rhyme characters and various animals whirled beneath the strobe lights, I caught sight of Lisa. She was dressed as a cat in a black leotard and tights, with a furry tail and a jewelled collar that glittered as she moved, and I smiled to myself at the aptness of the costume.

Unconsciously my gaze was searching the room for Greg, but so far I hadn't managed to pick him out.

Then I jumped as, above all the noise of the party, a voice behind me called out my name.

I whirled around, startled, and there

he was. Greg — only not Greg. He was almost unrecognisable. He'd darkened his face and was wearing a turban he'd twisted out of a crimson scarf, with a paste jewel at its centre. Standing with folded arms, and wearing narrow trousers and a Chinese-style silk dressing gown in glorious singing colours, he was an Indian prince, imperious, exotic and a total stranger.

I gasped. 'Wow! You look . . . *magnificent!*'

He laughed, his teeth gleaming very white against his dusky skin.

'You're looking pretty good yourself, Gipsy Rose,' he said, appraising my outfit. 'Are you going to tell my fortune, then?' He held out his open hand.

I took it and pretended to look at the lines, although my own hands were shaking so much that he must have noticed.

'Only if you cross my palm with silver, sir,' I replied archly, and backed off before I made a complete fool of myself.

Greg shrugged. 'Sorry, no cash,' he replied, and was turning away when I realised how brusque and standoffish I must have sounded. It was the last thing I had intended and I was desperately searching for a way to make amends when I caught sight of something that gave me an idea.

Quick as a flash I replied, 'Then I'll read this crystal ball for you instead, Your Highness,' and dropped him a mock curtsey. 'Would you take a seat, please?'

There were several small tables in an alcove nearby and I pulled out a folding chair for him.

In keeping with his character, Greg placed his palms together and bowed over them in acknowledgement.

On a window sill above, I'd spotted a couple of glass spheres which years ago had been fishing floats before the fisherman had started to use coloured plastic cones. Selecting one, I stood the 'crystal ball' in an ashtray to keep it steady and covered it with a gauze scarf

I'd had tied round my wrist.

I unhooked my bag from my shoulder and hung it on the back of my own chair as I sat down opposite Greg, for I'd filled it with small sprigs of 'lucky' heather to go with my costume and now its bulk was getting in the way.

It was slightly more quiet here in the alcove as we were partly shielded from the rest of the room by a couple of tall ferny pot-plants which also filtered the noise a little, so we could at least hear ourselves speak. It was, however, much darker, as the strobes didn't cover this corner and the only light came from one feeble spotlight high above.

'Right, Your Excellency,' I said as I removed the cloth from the glass sphere with a flourish and swirled my hands above and around it as I'd seen people do on TV. 'Gipsy Rose will see what there is to be seen.'

I leaned forward as if peering into its depth, then paused as I thought that here, surely, was a golden opportunity to find out more about this charismatic man and his secrets. If I could only draw him out . . .

'So,' I murmured, racking my brains for a clue as to how to begin, 'I see the sea.' That had to be a sure-fire certainty. 'I hear the pounding of the waves — ' perfectly true as the water outside was only a few yards away ' — and the sound of the rising wind.' I raised my eyes to Greg's face but it was inscrutable in the dark and impossible to gauge his reaction.

'There is a small boat, dwarfed by huge waves,' I went on, warming to my theme. He was a lifesaver, so . . . 'You are about to achieve a heroic rescue . . . ' I lowered my voice dramatically and went on, improvising for all I was worth.

'I see a body in the water, waving, crying for help . . . drifting farther away, but now — '

'*No!* No! Stop this! Stop it, do you hear me?'

My heart leapt with shock as Greg pounded his fist on the table, setting the whole thing rocking and making the 'crystal' leap from its stand. He jumped up, a movement so abrupt and so violent that his chair fell to the floor with a crash. Before I could react he pushed his way past me and was out through the crowds on the dance floor so swiftly that by the time I came to my senses and struggled after him, he was nowhere to be seen.

I staggered back into the corner and sank into my chair, covering my face with my hands. Whatever had I said to bring that on? Tears stung my eyes. How could what had started out as a light-hearted game have turned to such a nightmare in the space of a few short minutes?

★ ★ ★

'Good grief, Ginny, whatever happened there?'

I jerked my head up to see Janine standing over me with a look of concern on her face.

'I was waiting until you'd finished

with Greg, then I was going to have you tell *my* fortune, just for a bit of fun. Greg nearly knocked me over, he was in such a hurry to get away. What on earth did you *say* to him?'

The absurdity of her costume was so at odds with the seriousness of her face that I almost burst into hysterical laughter through the tears that were pricking my eyelids and the lump in my throat that felt as solid as a stone.

'I don't know.' I shook my head. 'I was only making up a bit of nonsense,' and I told her the story.

When I'd finished, however, she looked goggle-eyed at me for an instant, then clapped a hand over her mouth.

'Oh, Ginny, how could you be so stupid!' she exclaimed. 'Just as he was getting over all that at last — to go and remind him of it! No wonder he took it so badly. Poor Greg.'

Infuriated now, I sprang to my feet and grabbed her arm. 'Janine,' I said urgently, 'I've no idea what you're talking about. You've got to believe me,'

I went on giving her a shake. 'What is it that Greg's getting over?'

Seemingly genuinely shocked, her eyes locked with mine as she replied, 'You mean you really don't know? You've been here all these weeks and nobody's mentioned it?' She frowned. 'Of course, it was a couple of years ago now, but still . . . ' She bit her lip.

I gripped her arm more tightly. 'Tell me now, for goodness' sake,' I urged her.

'Well — ' Janine had just opened her mouth to begin when a piercing scream rang out from the other end of the room and echoed from the rafters.

'What on earth . . . ' she said as we both jumped in surprise.

The dancing was gradually coming to a halt as people turned to see what was happening. After a moment the group stopped playing as well and an uneasy hush fell over the place.

I was craning my neck along with everyone else, and in the distance I could see Lisa standing with one hand to her throat and a look of shock on her face.

'It's Lisa,' I said to Janine, who was too short to see for herself. 'I think it was her who screamed.'

Then Greg appeared at her side and held up a hand for silence.

'Sorry about this, folks,' he announced, 'but Lisa's lost her necklace. Could you clear the floor, please, and let's all try to find it? It shouldn't take long.'

As people began to shuffle their feet and withdraw to the sides of the room, heads bent to look at the floor as they went, Lisa was clinging to Greg's arm and sobbing.

'I b-borrowed it specially to wear tonight — it's a very valuable antique. Oh, what am I going to *do* if it doesn't turn up?'

'Calm down, Lisa,' said Greg with a touch of irritation in his tone as he patted her hand. 'We'll find it. You haven't been out of the room, have you?'

She shook her head and gulped.

'Well, there you are then, it can't have gone far, can it?' He stepped away from her. 'So if you all wouldn't mind having a good look around, please, then we can get on with enjoying ourselves.'

The Finger Of Suspicion

Half an hour later the wretched necklace still hadn't been found and in spite of their jolly costumes and painted smiles, I could sense that most of the crowd were feeling as fed-up as I was. Personally, I'd had as much as I could take of the evening. It had started out so light-heartedly in a bubble of happiness, which had now burst and left me deflated and with a sour taste in my mouth.

I was actually thinking of slipping away and going home when Greg rapped his knuckles on a table and waited again for silence to fall so that he could speak.

'I'm really sorry about this, everybody,' he said at last with a touch of embarrassment. 'As we seem to be getting nowhere with finding this wretched thing, Lisa has asked if you would all — if you wouldn't mind, that is — ' he swallowed and looked down at his feet ' — if you would turn out your pockets and bags.'

There came a chorus of disbelief before Greg repeated, 'I'm really sorry to have to ask this, but . . . ' He shrugged and spread his hands in a 'What can I do?' gesture.

'If you would each come up to the table in turn,' he suggested, 'and show Lisa that you've nothing to hide . . . It's unpleasant, I know, when we were having such a good time, but until this ghastly business is sorted out I'm afraid everybody will be under suspicion, you see?' he finished apologetically.

There were mutterings and murmurings of resentment and indignation as people started to form a line in front of Greg and Lisa, Greg giving a curt nod as each one shuffled by showing their opened bags and turned-out pockets.

I felt quite sorry for Greg — what an invidious position he was in. Lisa, red-eyed and snuffling, was slumped against his side now, clutching his arm with both hands, seemingly unable to support herself.

I sighed and went back to the corner to retrieve my own bag from where I'd left it and joined the queue behind Tony.

When my turn came I lifted my bag up on to the table and began pulling out all the sprays of heather. It took a minute or two to get rid of them, before I up-ended the bag and tipped out the rest of my belongings — comb, tissues, purse, and, to my embarrassment, all the clutter of old receipts and tickets and shopping lists which I'd been meaning to clear out for ages.

At the bottom there was something caught in one corner — something shiny that I didn't recognise. I frowned, gave the bag another shake, and to my horror out slipped the missing necklace.

The room tilted and I felt a roaring in my ears. Blindly I clutched at the back of a chair to steady myself as I swayed on my feet; I would have collapsed without it. In the background I heard a concerted 'O . . . Oh!' go up from the crowd, followed by a babble of voices, as I struggled to speak.

'But I didn't . . . ' My voice came out as a hardly audible croak. I licked dry lips and tried again.

'But I didn't take it!' I protested. 'Of course I didn't! It's all a mistake — an accident or something. Surely you believe me! You do — ' my voice faltered as I looked around at the blank, staring faces — 'don't you?'

There was an awkward pause full of shuffling feet as they glanced away, muttering amongst themselves, and I realised with dawning horror and a sick feeling in the pit of my stomach that not one person was going to utter a word of support for me.

I glanced around for Janine, the closest friend I had made round here, but she was nowhere to be seen.

Lisa had pounced on the necklace now and as her green eyes met mine I knew I was the only one to see the gleam of triumph in them. She'd set me up! And now she was going to make the most of it.

I stamped a foot as my control snapped and I saw red.

'You *planted* that on me,' I screamed at her.

'Oh, come on, Virginia,' she said, icily calm in the face of my unfettered temper, 'be reasonable. Why on earth should I?'

She gave a little titter and turned towards Greg, as sinuous as the cat she represented, and raised innocent eyes to his face.

'I've never heard such a feeble excuse in my life for being caught red-handed, have you, Greg?'

Turning her icy gaze back to me she pointed a finger and went on, 'You intended all along to steal it, else why did you stuff your bag with all this rubbish?' She ran a hand through the scattered sprigs of heather.

'How can you say that?' I retorted. 'It's obvious it's part of my costume!' I exclaimed, so incandescent with rage that I was shaking and my voice quivered. 'I had it with me before I even set eyes on your wretched necklace!'

Lisa raised her eyebrows and turned to Greg with a shrug.

'I wouldn't believe a word she says,' she remarked into his ear, but loud enough for me to hear, too. 'Ask yourself, Greg, how well do we really know her?' She glanced slyly at me. 'She comes down from up-country, worms her way in among us, ditches her own boyfriend and starts making up to you. You go out of your way to make her welcome — and then this is what she does in return.'

I hadn't dared look at Greg throughout all this, but when I did pluck up enough courage to do so I could see that his face was like granite and beneath the make-up his skin had paled. He was leaning over the table, gripping the edge of it so hard that his knuckles had whitened, and he was looking straight at me.

'Is that your only explanation, Virginia?' he demanded in a formal tone as if we were strangers, and when I nodded, I saw the disbelief in his eyes, swiftly followed by something that could have been hurt or disappointment.

'Of course it is,' I hissed, 'because there *isn't* any other. If *she*,' and I pointed a shaking finger at Lisa, 'didn't plant it on me, then someone else did.'

Greg frowned.

'But,' he said, seeming bewildered, and echoing Lisa's words, 'why should anyone want to? Where's the motive behind it?'

How I longed to tell him the truth: that Lisa had seen me as a rival for his affections and had deliberately set out to discredit me in public. But how could I? She had me in a corner and she knew it, hence that small, triumphant smile.

'I guess I must have made an enemy somewhere,' I replied, as I looked steadily in Lisa's direction.

When I looked back at Greg, it was to find him regarding me with a new hardness in his eyes, and in that instant I knew exactly what he was thinking. He knew the story of my background, and the words 'Like mother, like daughter' could have been written on his face.

Little knots of people were beginning to drift away now and leave the building, looking subdued and sickened by what had happened. The party was suddenly over, the group were packing up their instruments, the heart had gone out of the evening.

I felt sick myself as I scooped all the stuff back into my bag and prepared to follow them.

The heather sprigs I tossed into the nearest bin. A fat lot of luck they'd brought me, I thought, as my eyes pricked with tears, and I knew I would have to get out fast if I wasn't to break down in front of this objectionable woman. I wouldn't give her, or Greg either, the satisfaction of seeing how deeply I had been wounded by the incident.

I bit my lip to stop its trembling and crossed the room with my chin in the air and my head held high — so high that I almost bumped into Janine who was coming the other way.

* * *

'Ginny, are you all right?' she said as she caught sight of my face. 'You're as white as that wall. Has it got to you as well?'

I stared blankly at her. 'What? I don't know what you're talking about,' I replied, shaking my head.

She took my arm and drew me out on to the balcony.

'Oh, I must have eaten something dodgy at the barbecue,' she replied, leaning on the railings. 'I've spent the last twenty minutes in the toilet. What's happened to the party?' she asked, glancing at her watch. 'It's still early. Why is it all over?'

I let out a long, shuddering breath. 'Oh, Jan, you missed it all. There is so much you missed.' I rubbed both hands over my aching forehead and joined her with my elbows on the coping for support. 'Give me a minute and I'll fill you in.'

I took long, deep breaths of the pure night air and drank in the tang of salt and seaweed. The sea was very calm tonight, with little waves slapping half-heartedly at the sand as if they were too lazy to do more. The peaceful scene worked wonders as a restorative and when I'd composed myself I told her the whole story.

'I don't suppose you believe me either,' I said bitterly as I came to the end of the tale.

I stared at her, waiting for her expression to change to one of contempt as she disappeared out of the building like the rest of them.

'Oh, but I do,' she said and patted my arm.

Transfixed with amazement I could

only goggle at her.

'You d-do?' I stammered in disbelief and Janine nodded. 'But why . . . ? No-one else did . . . '

'Because,' she began to explain, 'I've been thinking as you were going through it all, and do you remember I told you how I was waiting until you'd finished telling Greg his fortune, so that I could have a turn myself?'

'Yes,' I said, frowning. 'Go on.'

'Well, I was standing behind those tall pot-plants, not wanting to listen to what you were telling Greg, and I saw Lisa hovering not far away. I didn't think anything of it, of course. She didn't see me, but I noticed her bend down and — I thought at the time — pick something up off the floor. It only took a second.' Janine looked at me and gestured with one hand.

'It was dim in that corner — you had your back turned and were concentrating on the crystal, and so was Greg. She could have been stooping to slip that necklace into your bag then. It was hanging off the back of your chair, do you remember?'

I felt my eyes widen and a broad smile spread across my face.

'Oh, Janine, you don't know what this means to me!' I exclaimed, throwing both arms around her. 'How wonderful it feels to find someone who believes I'm telling the truth. Oh, thank you — *thank you*.'

Then, to my embarrassment, the tears I had refused to shed in front of Greg and Lisa began to pour down my face, and my shoulders heaved in great sobs I could not control.

I rested my head on Janine's shoulder as she patted my back and made soothing noises until I'd recovered, then I scrubbed my eyes and gave her a tremulous smile.

'Sorry,' I said, 'for weeping all over your party frock.'

Janine turned down the corners of her baby-doll mouth and looked so comical that I burst out laughing.

'That's better,' she said approvingly,

then added in a more serious tone, 'Now, listen, what are we going to do about all this?'

She took a step or two and turned on her heel to face me again.

'I think Greg should be told,' she said decisively.

'No!' I shook my head, and she frowned.

'But, Ginny, you can't just let Lisa get away with it!'

'I don't want to, of course I don't, but can you imagine how pathetic it's going to sound? We haven't a scrap of proof — we can't pin a thing on her, she's been too clever for us. It's only your word against hers, Jan, and although it's wonderful that you would do this for me, and I can't tell you how grateful I am, I can't let you be humiliated as well.'

Janine had left my side and was pacing restlessly up and down the balcony with a frown on her face.

'I've been going over that moment in my mind, trying to remember if there was anyone else around at the same time who might have seen Lisa and could back us up, but I'm sure there wasn't.'

I shook my head. 'No. No-one said a word in there just now, and I'm sure they would have if they'd noticed her. I'm afraid we're going to have to sit tight and say nothing, Jan, however frustrating it is.'

'Where Do I Go From Here?'

I hardly slept at all that night. Images of the evening kept flashing through my mind like a video-replay and I only dozed off in a fitful slumber towards daybreak.

When I awoke again a couple of hours later, it was with the feeling that something bad had happened, but for a few seconds I couldn't recall what it was. Then the whole episode came flooding back and I groaned and buried my head in the pillow, wishing I could stay there for ever.

My mouth was dry though, and I had a thumping headache, and eventually I dragged myself out in search of some strong coffee, hoping it would cure both of these, and stared out over the bay as I sipped it.

It was still very early and the sun was just lightening the eastern sky, turning the bank of pearl-grey cloud to a milky blue and painting the tips of the waves with a delicate rose pink. It was going to be another lovely day, but for me it might just as well have been pouring with rain, in keeping with my spirits, which had sunk to an all-time low.

Where did I go from here? I heaved a sigh and slumped on to the padded window-seat. I might as well pack up and go home, there was no reason not to.

Looking back, though, what a life-changing experience these last few weeks had been. I'd broken up with Phil, and the full effect of that was still to hit me when I took up the threads of my 'real' life again. I'd discovered what I'd come here expressly to find out, my mother's story, and I was still trying to come to terms with the conflicting opinions about that — had she been a thief or hadn't she?

I'd had a great deal of fun for a while, until it had all gone sour. I'd met a man I would have liked to have known better, but now never would, and there was nothing left to keep me here any longer. Except that I'd promised Ruby Williams I would go and see her again. And I intended to. I'd liked the old lady and she'd been very kind and helpful to me. I couldn't just vanish without saying goodbye to her. Besides, it would give me something purposeful to do with the long day ahead.

Feeling better for having come to a decision, I made myself some toast and another mug of coffee. Then I dressed, and since it was still far too early to go visiting, I whiled away some of the morning by sorting my clothes and putting a load of them through the washing machine. I might as well take them home clean as dirty.

There was a line strung up at the back of the cottage and I pegged them out in the sun to dry. This was a novelty for me, as in London I'd only ever taken my washing out of the tumble dryer and aired it off indoors.

As I leaned on a wall and filled my lungs with the pure air, I was thinking how sweet my shirts would smell when they came in. How I was going to miss all this, I thought with a catch in my throat, as I gazed out over the sparkling sea, where the waves were now refracting bright shafts of the morning sunshine and tossing them high, before rolling up the beach in a welter of white foam. Like soapsuds, I thought irrelevantly, my mind still on the washing as I picked up the empty basket and turned to go indoors.

It was now almost mid-morning and by the time I'd driven into Hayle and bought a bunch of flowers for Ruby, it would be a respectable time to visit her.

★ ★ ★

I'd already knocked on the door and it was too late to go back, although I felt like fleeing down the path as quickly as I could as I suddenly remembered who had been here the last time I'd called.

What a fool I was — how could I have forgotten?

My heart began to thump nineteen to the dozen in the few moments it took Ruby to open the door.

'Ginny! Come in, my handsome. It's lovely to see you again.'

She stood back to let me in and I paused in the hallway, listening. The house seemed quiet enough — but he had been outside doing the garden, hadn't he? Perhaps I wasn't out of the wood yet.

I took a deep breath and handed over the flowers. 'These are for you,' I said.

'Oh, lilies — my favourites!' She buried her nose in a golden trumpet. 'What a heavenly scent. Thank you, my dear, very much.' Ruby turned and smiled over her shoulder as she led the way down to the kitchen saying, 'I must put these in water right away.'

'I'm the one to say 'thank you',' I replied, 'for all the help you gave me the other day, telling me about my mother.'

Ruby reached down a blue and white

china jug from the welsh dresser and filled it from the tap.

'Oh, it was a pleasure, dear. I'm always glad to have visitors. There's nothing better than a bit of chat over a cup of tea for cheering a body up, I can tell you.'

She arranged the lilies and stood them in the centre of the table.

'There, don't they look lovely?' She took another appreciative sniff, then went on, 'Yes, when you live on your own like I do, with no family, the days are sometimes long and it can get a bit lonely.' She turned and added over her shoulder, 'Especially when you're not feeling too well, you know?'

I nodded, looking at her with concern as she went on, 'I've been having the odd dizzy spell lately, and they frightened me a bit. But then,' and the cheerful smile was back on her face, 'we've all got something, I suppose. Doesn't do to dwell on things, does it?'

I made some sympathetic noises and asked her if she'd seen a doctor, but she shook her head and her face became set and solemn again as she avoided my eyes. I guessed she was more worried than she was letting on. Maybe she was afraid of seeking medical advice in case it turned out to be something serious.

I wondered if I ought to do anything about it — which would mean contacting Greg, of course, so I put the notion straight out of my head again. But not the person. I had to find out if he was likely to suddenly drop in.

'Does — um — Greg, your nephew, call in very often?' I asked casually, and waited in trepidation for her reply.

'Oh, Greg, yes. He's as good as gold, of course,' she replied fondly, 'but he has his job to go to, and all his spare time is spent out surfing — summer and winter, too.' She paused.

'Although I did wonder whether he would go on with it after the accident.' Ruby's face became serious and she gazed into space for a moment, tapping her fingers on the back of a chair.

'It took him a fair while, but this

summer he seems his normal self again,' she finally murmured.

'Accident?' I was all attention now. At last, here was an opportunity to learn about this mysterious accident that I'd heard about. Not that it mattered now, of course, but it would be interesting to hear what had actually happened.

'What sort of accident was that?' I enquired.

'You don't know?' Ruby's eyes widened. 'Oh, yes, well — I'll make a cup of tea and tell you all about it.'

She bustled across the room to put the kettle on, murmuring all the while to the ginger cat which had followed us into the house.

After making our tea she poured a saucer of milk for it and at last sat down. We were one each side of the range which at this time of the year was not lit, but it was obviously Ruby's habitual place.

'You don't mind staying in the kitchen, do you, dear?' she said. 'It's more cosy down here.'

Hastily I assured her that I didn't mind a bit, on edge with impatience as I willed her to get on with this story.

'Yes, well, it was like this, you see,' she began, raising her cup to her lips and taking a sip. 'One summer evening a couple of years ago, Greg was out surfing on his own — the lifeguards had left work, they finish at six — and he saw this couple climbing down the rocks towards the sea as if they were going swimming.' Ruby was gazing out of the window as if she could see it all for herself.

'Well, there was a strong rip current in that particular place and he pulled over to where they were and warned them how dangerous it was and that they shouldn't go in.'

'Greg said afterwards that the man was an arrogant know-all type who just swore at him and told him to mind his own business.' Ruby's face darkened. 'Pah — up-country people! Always think they know better than locals that have lived here all their lives.' Then she

149

gave me a startled look and clapped a hand to her mouth.

'Sorry, my handsome, I was forgetting you aren't from round here yourself. But you know I didn't mean you, don't you?'

'Of course I do, Ruby,' I reassured her. 'Anyway, I am *half* Cornish, aren't I?'

Ruby's eyes twinkled as she nodded and relaxed back in her cushioned chair, then picked up the story again.

'Anyway, apparently the woman was a bit more polite and thanked Greg, and as he was turning away he heard her trying to persuade the man not to go in the water — they were arguing away and he left them to it.'

'But Greg couldn't forget them and he said he kept glancing over that way from time to time as he was surfing, but he couldn't see them because of the pitching and tossing of the waves. Anyway, as he was standing on his board just about to come in, he suddenly heard screams, and saw the woman on the beach jumping up and down, frantically waving her arms and pointing out to sea.'

I could guess what was coming and my eyes never left her face as I listened to the drama unfolding.

★   ★   ★

'Well,' Ruby went on, draining her cup and placing it on the fender at her feet, 'Greg turned right round and headed back. He could see the man now and he was obviously in trouble, caught in the current, which was dragging him farther out.'

'Of course, Greg had to be careful not to be caught himself, so he tacked out as well as he could until he was within reach, shouting to the man not to panic.'

'But he *was* panicking — thrashing about and shouting for help, you know?' Ruby's eyes met mine.

'*Stupid* man!' I exclaimed and she nodded and pursed her lips.

'Anyway, Greg managed to swim up to the fellow and grab hold of him by his trunks, then tried to get him on to his surfboard, but he was a big chap and was making things harder than ever because he wouldn't help himself one bit. He was in such a state that he clutched hold of Greg and wouldn't let go, so Greg had to try to tow him in, using the board as a float for both of them.'

'Well, this worked all right for a while and they were rounding the bluff not far from the shore, almost within reach of safety, when the idiotic man reached out to grab hold of a spur of rock, apparently thinking he could climb on to it and save himself that way. Of course, he missed it and fell into the surging water, nearly taking Greg with him.'

Ruby spread her gnarled old hands expressively as she went on, 'Do you know what the surf's like under those cliffs? Pounding and sucking — there was no way Greg could get him out of that — those underwater rocks are wickedly sharp and it was too treacherous. He agonised over it, but knew that if he tried, then both of them would drown. So he made for the shore as quickly as he could to get help, and found that the woman had used her mobile phone and had already called the emergency services.'

'Greg was exhausted, of course, and just collapsed on the sand. He'd done all he could possibly do and risked his own life doing it, but by the time the rescue service arrived — ever so quick they were, too — the chap was dead. Heart failure, they said it was.' Ruby's face was solemn and drawn as she shook her head. 'Some job that was and I was some sorry for Greg.'

'A real hero, I called him, and so did a lot of other people,' she went on, 'but no matter what anyone said, he was terribly depressed afterwards, racked with guilt, blaming himself and saying it was his fault and that he'd failed the man. It's taken him all this time to get over it.'

'Mind you, I don't suppose he'll ever properly forget.' Ruby's gaze was far away again as her voice tailed away with the end of her story and we fell silent, each deep in our own thoughts.

I heaved a sigh. So, at last I knew. I knew why Greg occasionally withdrew into himself with that faraway, haunted look in his eyes. Knew why my stupid, stupid play-acting had touched on such a raw nerve.

I ground my nails into the palms of my hands and tried to block out the memory of the whole embarrassing incident, one part of me feeling almost glad that I would never have to face him again. But on the other hand . . .

I sighed and came back to earth.

I stood up to take my leave of her and she came down the passage to the front door to see me out. I was just going down the steps and had turned to wave to her, when I saw her stumble and catch at the doorframe for support. But to my horror she missed it, lurched to one side and before I could run back

154

to save her, the old lady had collapsed and was lying motionless on the tiled floor.

Imagining the worst, I ran to her side and felt for a heartbeat with hands that shook — but thank goodness, yes, she was alive.

I grabbed some cushions from the chair in the kitchen and placed them under her head, then went upstairs and ripped the duvet from her bed to make her as comfortable as possible before I called for the ambulance.

They arrived promptly in about ten minutes, by which time Ruby's eyes were flickering and she was showing signs of coming round. I squeezed her hand and tried to tell her what was going on, but doubted whether she could hear me.

As they were lifting her gently on to a stretcher, I explained what had happened, and also about the dizzy spells. One of them took it all down and also Ruby's details.

'Where are you taking her?' I asked

one of the men as they began to wheel the trolley toward the ambulance. 'A. and E. at Treliske Hospital,' he replied. 'You a relative of hers, are you, miss?'

'No,' I said. 'Well — yes, in a way — but I was just visiting.'

He gave me a peculiar look.

'Well, you'd better tell her next of kin,' he added, 'um — in case — you know?'

The ambulance drove away with his words echoing in my ears. Her next of kin. That had to be Greg, of course. Hadn't Ruby said he was her only relative? I would have to contact him. It was the last thing I wanted to do, but in the circumstances what choice did I have?

Ginny To The Rescue —Twice!

I phoned the library where Greg worked, not knowing his home number, and waited with my stomach full of butterflies as the girl on the other end went to look for him. But she returned full of apologies, saying that he had gone to headquarters in Truro for a meeting and could she take a message? Privately giving thanks, I said yes, she could, and told her what had happened.

Then, having done all that I could, I drove homewards almost on auto-pilot, unable to get Ruby out of my mind, and also what she had told me about Greg.

I was passing some shops when I jerked back to reality, remembering that I was almost out of basic groceries. If I was to eat during the few days left to me here, I needed to stop and get some things in. There was a mini-mart on the corner — that would do — and a space in the parking bay outside.

I filled a basket, added a magazine and the local paper for reading matter, and was through in a few minutes.

I ate my lunch in the open air, sitting on a sun-lounger in the tiny courtyard behind the cottage, which was bright with potted plants and heavy with the scent of a fragrant jasmine which had been trained up a wall on trellis, its starry white flowers nodding in clusters above my head.

Replete, I picked up the newspaper I'd bought and unfolded it. Not that the local news would be of much interest to me; I wondered really why I'd bought it at all, but there was an article about the seals and the disturbing virus which was still affecting them.

I turned a page and the headline here read, *Extraordinary Death-bed Confession of Octogenarian* followed by a longish column which I began to skim through out of idle curiosity.

Then my stomach did a somersault

and I jerked up into a sitting position as the content of what I was reading sank in.

I went back to the beginning and read it through a second time, more slowly, hardly able to believe my eyes.

It is reported that Mr Reginald Carpenter, it began, *who died this week on the eve of his eighty-sixth birthday, made an extraordinary last-minute confession to his family because, so he said, he wanted to clear his conscience before dying.*

Almost fifty years ago, he told them, he was guilty of stealing a sum of money from a firm where he was employed as a window-cleaner and has had it on his conscience ever since, although he was never suspected at the time.

Mr Carpenter stated that he had needed the money to take his desperately sick mother to America for some life-saving treatment which was unavailable in this country, and he succumbed to temptation. He then settled there with her for the rest of his life, only returning when he knew he had not long to live, and wanting to see Cornwall again before he died.

Once back here, he discovered that another employee of the firm, a young woman called Carrie, whose surname he never knew, had been accused of the theft and had unjustly been sent to prison for it.

This lady being subsequently deceased, Mr Carpenter wanted to put things right with her family in the event that any of them are still living in the area, and abjectly apologise for his crime, hoping that they will find it in their hearts to forgive him.

Therefore if anyone should recognise the story and know the identity of 'Carrie', the Editor invites them to contact this newspaper so that an old wrong may be publicly righted.

I let out all the breath I'd been holding in one long shudder, feeling as if someone had slapped me in the face. After all these years! Reg, the window-cleaner. So Sybil had been right in her suspicions.

Oh, poor Carrie! Tears were in my eyes and now began to stream down my face as the paper fell from my hand and the breeze tossed it around the courtyard unheeded.

I cried for Carrie, for my lost parents, for my failed partnership with Phil, for my faux-pas with Greg, and lastly for myself, wallowing in self-pity until I was cried out and exhausted. But I felt scoured by the storm of weeping, and cleansed by it, as if the public confession of the old man had at last put the seal of finality on my mother's story.

Now that her innocence was proven I felt as if a great weight had been lifted from my shoulders. I could close the file on my research now that I had discovered the last piece of the puzzle, and would be able to go home holding my head high on Carrie's behalf.

And would I contact the paper as the Editor asked? No. I wasn't looking for publicity. It was enough that I knew the truth for myself. Now that Carrie had been publicly vindicated there was nothing left to prove and no point in prolonging the story simply to sell more copies of the paper. No doubt there were plenty of other human interest pieces with which he could fill his columns. I was going back to London.

I couldn't stop thinking about Carrie's sad story, though, and having wandered aimlessly about the house for an hour, unable to settle to anything, I decided at last to go for a walk on the beach to clear my head.

★ ★ ★

Oh, my poor mother — to have had most of her short life blighted by such horrible circumstances. Now I could understand why my grandmother had been so negative about her — she had obviously believed her daughter-in-law guilty as charged.

I thrust my hands deep into the pockets of my shorts as I strode along, head bent against the stiff breeze that was blowing across the open bay, and still my restless mind would not be calmed. But at least my father couldn't have thought the same way as his mother; either that or he was so much in love that he was prepared to put it all behind them when he and Carrie were married.

I could imagine what rows there must have been when he announced that he was going to wed Carrie, and for the umpteenth time I wished I had known my parents. I truly hoped they had been happy for the couple of years they'd had together, and in their baby daughter — me — for the short time they'd known her.

Coming back to the present with a sigh, I found that I had walked further than I realised, right over to the far side where the sand gave way to a tumble of boulders and deep pools before forming a shelf of smooth flat rock which eventually became part of the towering cliffs high above.

It was very quiet here; the tide had receded to its lowest ebb, and the sun shone warmly on my face in the sheltered nook where I stretched out full-length on the shingle to rest and calm my racing thoughts.

I must have been more tired than I'd realised after my disturbed night, for I drifted off into a doze and slept soundly . . .

It must have been for some time, as I came round with a jerk, disorientated for a moment, with no idea where I was. The sun had gone behind a cloud and the breeze was cooler now. I rubbed the tops of my arms and shivered as I wondered what had woken me up so suddenly. Then I remembered that I'd had a creepy feeling that I was no longer alone, and shivered again as I scrambled to my feet and looked around.

The tide had come in considerably

further while I was sleeping and was now lapping at the shelf of flat rocks. I gasped, for if I'd been much longer it would have cut off my retreat.

Hastily I began scrambling back the way I had come, but then, from behind one of the larger rocks, I heard a most peculiar noise — a slithering sound, then a deep and long drawn-out moan like nothing I had ever heard before.

Rigid with terror, I felt goose-pimples break out on my skin and the back of my neck began to prickle.

I stood stock-still, rubbing clammy hands down my sides, and tried to swallow on a throat gone suddenly dry.

As I waited for the other person to appear, I looked frantically this way and that for a means of escape — but I was trapped between the sea and the cliffs with only the one narrow passage out between the rocks. There was no way I was going to avoid this encounter. I could only wait with my heart in my mouth for whatever might come.

But nothing did. I stood for several

minutes, shaking with fright, until at last the moaning noise came again, louder and longer than the previous time. And now it suddenly reminded me of something. I heard Greg's voice again, on the day we'd gone out in the boat to see the seals and he had been talking about the weird noise they made. I could even remember his exact words . . . 'a deep, moaning kind of boom that echoes up the cliff and can give you goose-pimples if you don't know what it is . . .'

That was it. And here I was with the goose-pimples, too!

Now I had a good idea who my terrifying companion was, but I took a deep breath and consciously plucked up my courage in case I might be wrong after all, before I headed round the large rock where the sound had come from.

It *was* a seal, of course, a half-grown one by its size. A lovely dappled grey in colour, it was lying on a flat rock, its head up, looking straight at me.

I took a step closer, then gasped, for it was obviously very sick. Its huge, beautiful eyes were dulled and gummy and its breathing was laboured and seemed to be causing it pain.

Rooted to the spot, I wondered what best to do.

'Don't approach one if you find it,' John had said. 'You'll frighten it off and it'll try to get back to the water. We'll lose sight of it and it'll probably die.'

So I must go for help — and quickly, before the tide reached the poor creature.

I sprang into action, scrambling over the rocks as fast as I could, and ran back over the sand towards the life-guards' headquarters. Someone there would know what to do. And as I ran I was thanking the fates for making this a working day, and Greg safely out of the way in Truro.

I panted up the steps to the building and bent over double for a moment, my hands on my hips as I fought to regain my breath. And when I straightened up, there he was, looming over me.

I felt all the colour drain from my face.

'Greg!' I stuttered. 'Oh! But I thought . . . '

I was clearing my throat to continue when Greg, looking as astonished as I was, said, 'Ginny! What on earth . . . is something wrong?' He gazed curiously at me as I struggled to compose myself.

I nodded and pointed down the beach.

'A sick seal,' I blurted out, 'on the rocks, around the point — over there. Quick — we must rescue it! The tide's coming in fast.'

'Oh, right, I see.' He seemed to pull himself together and reached in a pocket for his mobile phone. After a few seconds I heard him talking to John and giving him directions.

'He'll be along in a few minutes,' he said, 'with the rescue crew and a cage to put the poor creature in. How bad is it, could you tell?'

I swallowed and shook my head. 'Not

really,' I replied. 'It was moaning and having trouble breathing. But it looked like a young one and seemed quite fat and well-nourished, you know?'

Greg nodded. 'Good. In that case, maybe it'll be OK. You'll have to come and show them exactly where it is. We'll take the buggy. Come on.'

I followed him down the beach to where a quad bike stood beside the canoes and boards in readiness for emergencies.

'Hop in,' Greg said, revving the engine, and I slipped into the seat behind him.

We were off in a moment, hurtling over the wide, firm expanse of sand by the water's edge. It was completely exhilarating, the nearest thing to flying I had ever experienced.

I gasped as the wind streamed through my hair and swept my breath away, and clutched at the tail of Greg's tee-shirt to steady myself. But when the machine bucked over a ridge of sand and I was almost dislodged, this wasn't enough and I was forced to put my arms around his waist and hold on for dear life.

In this position the side of my face came naturally to rest on Greg's warm back, where I could feel the ripple of every muscle as he manoeuvred the machine. The sensation was almost as unsettling as the ride, and my body was responding in ways I didn't want to think about, so that as we slowed down and the bike came to a halt at the far side of the beach I didn't know whether to be glad or sorry.

I climbed down, slightly dazed, while Greg took out his mobile and was contacting John again, giving him directions.

'You'd better park just above the dunes, mate,' I heard him say. 'You'll have to do the rest on foot. Down that narrow track and over the rocks to the right. We'll meet you there.'

He put the phone away and turned to me.

'Right, show me where it is.'

We scrambled over the rough ground and around the point to where I'd seen the seal.

'This is as far as we'd better go,' I said, 'or we'll frighten it. Oh, I hope the poor thing's still alive.'

Just then we heard its moaning cry and I relaxed.

'There!' I exclaimed. 'It's behind that big black rock — can you see the one I mean?'

Greg nodded and turned away to scan the cliffs, shading his eyes with a hand.

'Ah, here they come,' he said as, following his pointing finger, I could make out some tiny figures descending the cliff face.

Soon the rescue party had joined us, two men with a cage like a huge cat-basket and a woman with a bundle of towels under her arm. She saw me staring at them and smiled.

'A seal's a slippery creature,' she explained. 'It's hard to get a grip, especially when it's frightened and struggling. I'm going to hold it still while we give it a tranquillising jab, then we can get it into the cage.'

They crept slowly around the rock and out of sight . . .

★ ★ ★

Soon the job was done and they were manhandling the cage up the cliff, to where John was waiting in the van, and we saw them drive away.

Our own ride back was a far more leisurely affair than the outward one had been, and I sat sedately on the seat without needing any support. The other experience seemed like a dream, and facing Greg's rigid spine now I wondered if I had actually been fantasising.

Greg returned the buggy to its position on the beach and I followed him into the lifeguards' station.

'Phew,' he exclaimed, rasping a hand over his jaw, 'it's been quite a day. I got your message about Aunt Ruby but haven't had a chance to talk to you — Ginny, thank you so much for what you did.'

We were climbing the stairs and as he turned his eyes met mine and locked for a moment.

He was wearing a bright blue polo shirt which reflected and enhanced the vivid blue of his eyes. With his fair hair bleached by sun and sea-water and his glorious golden tan, he looked like some Scandinavian god, and my heart turned over with a familiar flutter again.

'It could have been so much worse if she'd been on her own.'

I shrugged and looked away.

'It was just luck that I happened to go round there at the right time.'

'I called in at the hospital on my way home from the meeting,' Greg went on. 'It was over by lunchtime and I thought I'd take the rest of the day off — get in a bit of surfing. They owe me a couple of hours overtime, so it seemed like a good opportunity.'

'Oh, how is Ruby now?' I asked

eagerly. 'Were you allowed to see her?' Conversation was becoming easier now that we had a common topic to discuss.

'Let's sit down,' Greg said, 'and I'll tell you. You look exhausted.'

I suddenly realised how right he was. All the emotional stuff as well as the sprint across the beach had taken its toll and I felt ready to drop.

Greg indicated a table by the window and a nearby drinks machine.

'Coffee? Tea?' He raised an eyebrow.

'Oh, coffee would be lovely,' I replied, fishing in my bag for a coin, but he waved it away.

I gazed out of the window and across the sand to the water's edge. Two of the lifeguards were moving the red and yellow flags which indicated safe bathing and carrying them up the beach as the tide came further in, while some others moved the surf boards and canoes which were always positioned in readiness for an alert.

Greg was soon back with two paper cups and our conversation resumed.

'So, yes,' he said, lowering himself into one of the small wooden chairs at the table and folding his long legs away, 'I was allowed to look in on Aunt Ruby and she was delighted to see me, of course. She looked very pale and shocked — obviously she'd had a terrific fright, but she was in quite good spirits. I managed to find the doctor who'd been attending her and had a word with him before I left.' He paused and took a swig of his coffee.

'Oh, that's so good,' he said and leaned back in his chair. 'I missed lunch — no time — and I guess I've been running on empty for a couple of hours!'

He smiled and although it was a smile that did not reach his eyes, I felt the tension in my muscles ease a little. Our initial awkwardness had lightened slightly and I politely returned the smile.

'They've done some X-rays. Apparently she's broken a small bone in her ankle. The doctor said that she's very shocked, and bruised as well, of course, but for her age she's standing up to it pretty well. They were just going to put her leg in plaster when I left. He was very interested to hear about the dizzy spells, though.'

Greg put his cup down and face was full of concern as he leaned across the table.

'Ginny, do you know, she never once mentioned to me that she'd been having dizzy spells? I suppose it's because she knew I would have made her see a doctor right away. So that's something else I have to thank you for, else the medics would never have known either.'

I raised my palms in a dismissive gesture.

'I guess she's one stubborn and independent old lady,' I replied.

Greg twirled a spoon in the last of his coffee then drained it.

'Mm. They suspect it's high blood pressure that's causing the dizziness,' he explained as he crumpled up the empty cup and tossed it into a nearby bin, 'which can apparently be controlled with medication and diet.'

'Well, a broken ankle is bad enough, of course, but I'm very glad it's no worse,' I replied. 'I was imagining all sorts when she was just lying there with her eyes shut.'

Greg nodded. 'It must have given you quite a fright,' he said, giving me an understanding look that set the hairs on my arms prickling. His hand was almost touching mine and it felt like a magnet, so without making it too obvious I moved mine further away.

'Poor Aunt Ruby. She's been very good to me,' Greg said, gazing out of the window. 'When my parents broke up — I was sixteen then and it was the worst upheaval of my life — she was always there for me, you know?'

I nodded and tried to imagine him at sixteen, a lonely boy whose world had been turned upside down.

'Actually I lived with her for a few years after that,' Greg went on, 'and she kept me from going off the rails, which I could easily have done. So I'd like to repay a bit of that by looking out for her now that she's helpless. I really can't thank you enough for what you did, Ginny,' he repeated, as our eyes met.

I looked down and traced a pattern in some grains of spilt sugar as I said softly, 'Well, I'm fond of Ruby, too, you know. She does happen to be my relation as well, don't forget.'

Then I raised my head as practical matters took over.

'I wonder how long she'll be in hospital?' I remarked. 'I must go and visit her before I go home.'

'Home? Oh, yes, of course,' Greg said shortly. 'They did mention three or four days, depending on how she gets on. When are you leaving?' he asked.

I wondered why he should be interested — or more likely he was just being polite.

'At the end of this week,' I replied. 'The let on the cottage runs out then.'

Greg nodded, then gave me a long

and calculating look.

'And when does your school term start?'

I raised an eyebrow. What was all this?

'In two weeks' time.'

He nodded again and the conversation turned back to Ruby.

'I'm very worried about how she'll manage when she comes out of hospital,' Greg said, frowning. 'She's not going to be able to do a thing for herself with her leg in plaster. And I have to go to work — I've taken all my leave for this year and they're short-staffed as it is.' He nibbled his bottom lip.

'I'll have to contact the social services and get something organised, but that takes time. Unless . . . ' He paused and there was the calculating stare again, and the frown.

Suddenly the penny dropped and I knew exactly what he was thinking. Then I felt my eyes widen and my mouth drop open in astonishment as the implications sank in. I swallowed hard.

'Greg, do you mean — are you thinking — that I should . . . ?'

'Why not?' he countered defensively. 'As you said yourself, Ruby is your relation as well.' He obviously wanted to make it clear that he wasn't begging me for any favours. Then he spread his hands wide.

'Ginny, is there any reason why you couldn't stay on for another week or so and move in with her temporarily? It would give me a breathing space and time to get some professional help sorted out.' I noticed that he had pointedly avoided saying 'please', although by the note of pleading in his voice it was apparent that he was desperately hoping I would agree.

My mind had switched to overdrive. This sudden reversal of what I'd been taking for granted — that the let had run out therefore I had to go home — had completely thrown me and my thoughts were in turmoil. And Greg's fixed blue gaze was not making it easy to concentrate.

I swallowed hard.

'I — I . . . well, actually — no, I suppose not. No, there isn't,' I heard myself stammer. And from that moment I knew I was committed.

Oh, well, it could be worse, I told myself. There was really nothing much to go home for in the short term, and it would postpone my meeting with Phil, which was bound to be difficult. I would have company, even if it was only a handicapped old lady, and could enjoy Cornwall for a little bit longer.

Taking Care Of Ruby

So a couple of days later, after Greg had discovered that Ruby would be coming out at the weekend, I packed up my things and moved into her home, to be there when she arrived. There was very little to do — Ruby kept her house immaculately clean and tidy, and apart from shopping for food, my time was my own.

So, after unpacking my few belongings and making up a bed for myself in the spare room, I wandered out into the tiny garden at the back of the house.

It was mostly grass, with a few flowering shrubs and a couple of tubs filled with bright bedding plants, but, like everything else about Ruby's home, it was immaculately tended.

I was on my way back in when a voice called 'Cooee!' and I turned to see a female face with a friendly smile peeping over the wall that divided Ruby's garden from the one next-door. Then, as she hoisted herself up to stand on something and the rest of her appeared, I felt my jaw drop in amazement.

'Janine!' I exclaimed, at the same time as she said, 'Ginny! What on earth are you doing here?'

We both burst out laughing and I explained the situation.

'So she's your aunt, too — Mrs Williams — as well as Greg's. Why didn't you say so before?'

'Well, the subject never came up. I could just as well ask you why you didn't tell me where you lived! And Ruby's not an aunt exactly — second cousin, I suppose you'd call her,' I replied, and spread my hands as I tried to explain.

'Anyway, how is she? And what's the matter with her? I heard she'd gone into hospital — somebody saw the ambulance — but I was away at work myself, so I didn't know anything about it until I came home that night.'

I told Janine the details of what had happened.

When I came to the end of my tale she said, 'Tell her that Horace is all right, will you? I expect she's been worrying about him. But I've been feeding him these last few days.'

I looked blankly at her. Horace?

'The cat,' Janine said, and my hand flew to my mouth.

'Oh! I'd completely forgotten about him,' I exclaimed, as a vision of the little ball of ginger fur stretched out on the garden wall came back to me. 'And Greg never said — oh, that was good of you. Thanks ever so much. Where is he now?'

'Oh, he does his own thing,' Janine replied. 'He's quite friendly with my own cat — they go off hunting together sometimes. He'll come home when he's hungry again. But hey, why are we standing out here? Why don't you come round and have a cup of coffee with me while you're waiting for Mrs Williams?'

So I did that. We had a companion-able drink together and Janine showed me round her tiny house, of which she was obviously very proud.

'The mortgage keeps me poor,' she said, 'but it's worth it to have my own place.'

'And to be able to look out at all this every day, too!' I exclaimed, as I leaned out of the open sash window in her bedroom, breathing in the sea air and admiring the fantastic view over the estuary. The tidal river was winding its way from the harbour through a deep channel which cut across the wide sweep of amber sands to enter the sea, and a small fishing boat was put-putting its way towards St Ives. What a wonderful place to live, I thought with a wistful sigh, thinking of the bustle, noise and stress which awaited me at home.

* * *

So Ruby returned home in a wheel-chair, and after a day or two had learned how to get about slowly and laboriously with a walking frame. I admired the old lady's courage — she was obviously tougher than she appeared. Greg had arranged her bed downstairs for her temporarily and she accommodated herself to her disability remarkably well.

'They say I'll be getting this thing off in a week or so,' she said, pointing to the plaster cast, 'then they'll give me something lighter to wear.'

I was standing at the sink drying the breakfast dishes, and looked over my shoulder with a smile.

'That'll be good,' I said, 'although you're doing pretty well as you are.'

Ruby nodded and looked fondly at me.

'But that's all thanks to you, my handsome. I couldn't manage without you to help me get dressed, and to do all the shopping and cooking. I'm more grateful than I can tell you for staying on like this.'

'Nonsense,' I replied, putting the

crockery away in an overhead cupboard. It was taking me a while to find out where everything went, and Ruby was a stickler for neatness and order. The saying 'A place for everything and everything in its place' could have been written specially for her.

'It's a pleasure,' I replied, which was true, as Ruby had been telling me all sorts of interesting things about her childhood, and some of her anecdotes included little snippets about my mother.

'And it gives me an extended holiday, doesn't it?' I added.

'How I shall miss you when you go back though.' Her eyes clouded and her forehead puckered.

'By that time,' I said briskly, 'you'll be a lot better, and Greg's going to get help for you from the social services. They'll take over where I leave off. You'll get meals delivered, someone will come night and morning — you'll be waited on like royalty!' I joked, in an attempt to reassure her.

I was hanging the tea-towel up to dry when I suddenly remembered something.

'Oh!' I exclaimed. 'I nearly forgot — I've got something to show you. I'll just run upstairs and fetch it. Shan't be a minute.'

I'd saved the newspaper cutting about Carrie in case Ruby had missed it. Obviously she had done, else she would have mentioned it by now.

'Look at this,' I said, as I thrust it into her hand and found her reading glasses.

She took some time, carefully reading every word, then, 'Well, bless my soul!' she said as she came to the end. 'Who'd have thought it — after all this time, to find out what actually happened! What a horrible man he must have been to keep something so important to himself all these years. Oh, Ginny dear, you must be so thrilled.'

Ruby actually had tears in her eyes as she carefully folded the piece of paper and handed it back.

'I am,' I said simply. 'It seems like the last piece of the jigsaw. The end of the story that I came down here to find.'

'And are you going to contact the newspaper, dear?' Ruby looked enquiringly over the top of her glasses.

'No,' I replied, shaking my head. 'It's nobody else's business but ours. I don't want Carrie's story plastered all over the Press. It's too personal.'

Ruby nodded. 'I'm so glad that's the way you feel, because so do I. Far better to draw a line under it. It's all over and done with now,' she said firmly, 'and Carrie can rest in peace.'

We both fell silent for a minute, lost in our own thoughts, before I shook myself back to the present.

'Now, what would you like to do this morning — sit in the garden?' I suggested, 'It's a lovely day.'

Ruby glanced out of the window.

'All right, dear, I'll take my knitting and the newspaper and you can leave me and go off somewhere if you want to. There's no need for you to be tied to the house all the time.'

My spirits lifted as I heard this.

'Are you sure you'll be all right?' I said with concern. But I *had* begun to feel cooped-up in the tiny house; I hadn't been further than the corner shop for days. I was longing for a good walk, and looking out over such a tempting view all the time didn't help.

'Of course I shall,' Ruby replied stoutly. 'Can't come to much harm in the back garden, can I?'

'Well, I will go for a walk then — a short one, just down to the sea, after I've got you settled. I'll be about an hour, OK?'

I gathered up her knitting, a magazine and the daily paper, found her spectacles and pushed the chair through to the garden, then made a quick cup of tea and took that out to her, too.

'My goodness, but you're spoiling me,' Ruby said with a smile. 'I'll not be letting you go at the end of this week! But you've done enough for me now — off you go and have your walk. And don't think you've got to hurry back — I'll be fine here,' she insisted.

★ ★ ★

The tide was way out and I scrambled down over the dunes towards it — 'the towans', they were called locally, blown heaps of sand colonised by marram grass and a huge variety of wild plants, some of which grew nowhere else.

As I slipped and slid on the dry powdery sand to the bottom, the wind blew the scent of salt and sea in my face and the sun was warm enough on my back to penetrate the thick cotton of my polo shirt.

It was a long walk out to the tide's edge, over firm, even sand dotted with tiny shells and blown seaweed. I took off my sandals and let my feet crunch across it, and splashed through small pools which reflected the azure sky and had been warmed by the sun until they felt like a tepid bath.

Reaching the water, I paddled along in the crisp little waves at its edge, letting them beckon me onwards until I realised I'd walked almost as far as

191

Gwithian, the next cove along the coast. I glanced at my watch. Yes, it was time to turn back if I was to be home within the hour, as I'd promised.

I left the water and began to retrace my steps.

The climb back up the sand-hills seemed to take forever; my feet constantly slid away, and for every one step forward I seemed to take two back.

At last, panting, I reached the top of one of the firm grassy tracks which criss-crossed the hills in all directions. I paused to catch my breath and walked a few steps backwards as I took one last glance at the glorious view.

Sadly that was my undoing, for my foot caught in a rabbit-hole as I turned and in a second I had stumbled and fallen, giving my knee a nasty wrench which made me cry out in pain and brought tears to my eyes.

I sat there for a moment nursing my leg and calling myself all sorts of a fool for not taking more care.

But I had to get going. The pain did

seem to be easing a little so maybe I hadn't done too much damage to my knee. It would be ironic, I thought darkly, if I'd stayed here to help Ruby out and had crippled myself as well.

I looked around, but there was no-one about. There never is when you need help, is there, although on the way out there had been a whole lot of people walking dogs and taking their children down to the beach.

I levered myself to my feet and tested my knee. It hurt, but not excruciatingly. Maybe it was just bruised, I thought hopefully, and began to hobble along. As I went it didn't seem to get any worse, but I had to stop and rest every so often and consequently was much later getting home than I'd promised. I shrugged — Ruby of all people would understand that accidents happen.

*   *   *

Eventually I reached the house and went straight round the corner to the garden, calling out to Ruby that I was back. There was no reply, however, and when I reached the lawn there was no sign of her.

I went into the house through the back door, calling her name, but there wasn't a sound here either.

I limped upstairs, although common sense told me she couldn't possibly be there, and indeed she wasn't.

Shock rooted me to the spot. Ruby had gone — disappeared, vanished, wheelchair and all. What on earth had happened?

Standing there on the verge of panic, I forced myself to take a deep breath, calm down and think logically. There was no way Ruby could have gone far on her own, therefore someone must have taken her. And who could that someone be? It had to be him, didn't it? Greg — 'my favourite nephew'.

I stopped being anxious as fury took over.

Going through the house to the front door, I flung it open to look up and down the street. And in the distance there they were, coming up the hill, Greg pushing the wheelchair and both of them laughing at some joke as Ruby waved a hand to a group of her neighbours on the corner.

I met them on the doorstep with a face I knew was as thunderous as I felt.

'Hello, dear,' Ruby said cheerfully. 'I hope you weren't worried about me, but Greg called and when you didn't get back within the hour like you said, we didn't wait any longer for you. He took me on a lovely walk, right the way down the river. I really enjoyed the outing.'

Fond as I was of Ruby, at that moment I could have smacked her for wrong-footing me so. I'd offered several times to take her out in the chair but she would never let me — she'd always said she was perfectly happy to stay in the garden. Then to point out to Greg that I'd been late back, whether she'd meant it that way or not, made me seem neglectful, and consequently I was now feeling more furious than ever.

'Of course I was worried about you,' I retorted sharply, replying to Ruby but looking directly at Greg. 'How do you think I felt, with you nowhere to be seen? I've been imagining all sorts of things that could have happened to you.'

'Oh, well, nothing did, as you can see! Here we are again and no harm done, eh?'

The old lady propelled herself towards the kitchen and I was left standing in the hall beside Greg.

'Couldn't you at least have had the sense to leave a note?' I hissed under my breath as I glowered at him.

'I'd say I displayed just as much sense as you did in not coming back when you'd promised,' he said blithely, and quirked an eyebrow. 'A fine carer you turned out to be,' he added with a grin.

It was said jokingly but the remark stung, and I nibbled my lip to bite back foolish tears as I fought against the urge to tell him *why* I'd been delayed. But if he wasn't concerned enough to ask, my pride wasn't going to let me justify myself to him; it would only sound as if I was making excuses.

So I swept past him with my chin in the air and followed Ruby into the kitchen.

* * *

As Greg helped her out of the wheelchair and handed her the walking frame, Ruby said, 'Well now, young man, are you going to stay and have some lunch with us? It's only sandwiches and salad, isn't that right, Ginny?' I nodded as she went on, 'But there's plenty if you want to.'

'Right, I'll do that.' Greg perched a hip on the corner of the table and swung a long leg to and fro. 'Then I'll trim those bushes out the back this afternoon, before I go down to the beach. OK?'

'Lovely, dear,' Ruby said over her shoulder as she made her way out of the room towards the downstairs toilet.

Ignoring my throbbing knee, I started banging about preparing lunch as Greg poked around in the drawers of the dresser and put out cutlery and table mats.

'Why are you limping?' he asked after a moment's silence.

Having had my back towards him as I started work on the sandwiches, I hadn't known he was watching me and I jumped in surprise as he spoke.

'Oh — oh, I had a tumble and wrenched my knee — just now, while I was out,' I said casually, buttering bread. I turned towards the sink to wash lettuce, but he came up behind me and took it out of my hands.

'I can do that,' he said firmly. 'Sit down and let me have a look at that knee.'

'No! No — it's nothing, I just twisted it a bit, that's all.' But Greg's hands were pressing me firmly down into one of the wooden kitchen chairs then lifting my leg on to another.

His golden head was very close to my face as he bent over, and I caught a whiff of fragrant aftershave, something spicy and crisp. Mm, nice, one part of my mind was saying, as the other was registering the strong, warm clasp on my knee as he gently manipulated it.

'Mm, I think it's only bruised,' he said at last, 'but you ought to rest it as much as you can.' He straightened up. 'Now, you stay there — I can perfectly well make a few sandwiches — '

'But — ' I protested and he held up a hand.

'But nothing, I mean it. Now, where's the salad shaker?'

As he busied himself in my place he went on over his shoulder, 'There's some good stuff down in the lifeguards' place that we use for sprains and strains. It's specially made for sports injuries. I'll bring some round later.'

'Th — thank you,' I was saying in a subdued tone, when he suddenly stopped as if a thought had struck him and turned back to face me, a knife poised in his hand.

'Is that why you were late back?

Because of the knee?' he demanded. 'It is, isn't it?'

I looked down at the floor and nodded.

'You silly idiot!' he exclaimed. 'Why didn't you say so? You mean to say you took all that flack from me and never said a word?' His face was a picture of contrition and there was a softness about his eyes I'd never seen before.

I shrugged as words failed me, and I could have sworn he was muttering something under his breath that sounded like, 'Oh, you poor little thing,' but I couldn't be sure because at that moment Ruby flung the door open and came thumping back into the room.

Greg began explaining the situation and I tried to protest to Ruby that I was all right as she started clucking like a mother hen, and eventually we got around to eating lunch.

★　★　★

As the three of us sat around the table like a small family, the situation seemed slightly unreal — surreal almost — when I considered the yawning divide which lay between Greg and myself.

Ruby kept the conversation going with trivialities, and also told Greg about the newspaper story which vindicated Carrie after so long.

He seemed to be as thrilled as I was to have the mystery cleared up, and looked at me long and hard as Ruby came to the end.

After we'd finished lunch she went off for her afternoon lie-down and Greg and I between us cleared up the dishes.

It seemed very quiet after Ruby had gone and we were left working together. To an outsider we would have looked like the best of friends.

For the sake of saying something to break the silence, I remarked, 'Ruby's been telling me how much you do for her — even before this accident — in the garden and so on. She's very proud of you, Greg.'

He snorted and shrugged his shoulders but I soldiered on.

'In fact, she was telling me about the — um — that tragedy in the water and singing your praises, saying how brave you'd been . . . '

'That's rubbish!' he retorted, whirling round at me, and suddenly his eyes were blazing with emotion and his mouth was set in a tight line.

'Ruby exaggerates. *Brave* you call it?' He flung a handful of cutlery down on the draining board with a clatter. 'For goodness' sake — the guy *died*, didn't he?' His hands were gripping the edge of the sink so hard that his knuckles had whitened.

'But you risked your own life!' I protested, gathering up the scattered knives and forks and drying them. 'You could have died, too,' I added softly, resisting the urge to clasp one of those hands comfortingly in my own.

'Greg, it wasn't your fault that the man had a dodgy heart. You did your utmost — no-one could have done more.'

He growled and muttered, splashing about in the washing-up bowl.

I cleared my throat and said tentatively, 'Greg, I'm — er — so *sorry* about that silly fortune telling thing. Believe me, I didn't know about all that at the time . . . or I would never have dreamed . . .'

'Oh, forget it,' he snapped, waving a dismissive hand, and emptied the bowl. He dried his hands and went to stand by the window with his fists thrust deep in his pockets and his back to me as he gazed out over the garden.

I guessed he was thinking the same as I was — about what had happened afterwards.

In the silence that had now fallen, the friendly atmosphere suddenly cooled as things *not* said loomed between us like the shadow of an insurmountable wall, and I wondered miserably if that business would ever be resolved.

I didn't want to leave Cornwall with a slur on my name, but on the other hand, why on earth would it matter so much? I knew in my own heart that I was innocent and that was the most important thing of all. Wasn't it?

The Heart's Truth

Greg spent an hour or so tidying the garden while I kept well out of the way, finding jobs to do around the house until he'd gone.

I'd forgotten all about the medication he had said he'd bring back, and was changing the duvet cover on Ruby's bed when I heard his voice asking her where I was.

'Come outside,' he said with a jerk of his head as we met in the hall. 'This stuff is very efficient, but it smells appalling — Ruby won't want it stinking her house out.'

I smiled.

'OK,' I replied and followed him through the back door.

As I subsided into a garden chair I held out my hand for the ointment. There was no way I was going to have him handling my leg again, it was far too disturbing.

'Oh, it doesn't smell that bad,' I remarked, as I smoothed it on, and raised my eyebrows in surprise.

I was even more surprised when I noticed that Greg, who was sitting in the other one of the pair of chairs, was regarding me with a strange expression that I couldn't quite fathom. If I hadn't known better I would have thought it was embarrassment, but that, of course, was utterly ridiculous.

'No,' he said, 'it doesn't. That was just an excuse to get away from Aunt Ruby.'

He paused, his forearms resting on his knees; he was rubbing his hands together as if he didn't quite know what to do with them.

'Um, Ginny,' he said, not meeting my eyes, 'there's something I have to say to you.'

'Oh?' I felt my eyes widen and my hand paused with the tube of ointment poised as I waited for him to go on.

'It's quite a long story, actually.' He

cleared his throat and took a deep breath.

'When I went down to the headquarters just now I met our caretaker, Bob, and we got talking. He'd been looking out for me for days apparently, to tell me something, but we kept missing each other.'

I waited, saying nothing as Greg went on.

'It — um — goes right back to the night of the party, actually.'

Head bent, he was studying his trainers as if he'd never seen them before. My heart began to beat a little faster as I wondered what was coming.

'Bob came round to see if the party was over so that he could lock up, you see,' Greg murmured. 'And on the way in he stopped at the bottom of the stairs to tidy up some boards and canoes and stuff which had fallen out of one of the cupboards. He's very safety conscious and he was worried that someone might fall over them.'

I nodded, remembering. I'd noticed

those bits of kit all over the floor myself, when I'd come in.

My gaze was fixed on Greg's bent head as he took another breath.

'Anyway, that's all by the by. The point is, Bob could see up the stairs to where we were sitting, you and I, as you were telling my fortune. And he noticed Lisa creep up, all furtive like, looking over her shoulder as if she wanted to make sure there was no-one watching — and he saw her slip something into your bag. Something that glittered as it caught the light, he said.'

My stomach lurched and did a somersault while Greg absently scuffed one foot in the grass and avoided looking at me. The silence was deafening.

Eventually he cleared his throat again and continued.

'He went back home when he realised the party obviously wouldn't be over for some time — and he only lives a stone's throw away, you see — then he came back much later to lock up when we'd all gone. But the impression that Lisa had been up to no good stayed with him.'

'Anyway,' at last Greg straightened up and our eyes met, 'it was days before he heard about what had happened, and of course, when he did, he realised what he'd seen. Ever since then he's been looking for me to tell me what he saw.'

'Ginny, what can I say?' Looking extremely uncomfortable, he spread his hands wide.

I wasn't going to help him — some little devil in me was saying let him squirm for a bit — so I just shrugged and said nothing. But at that moment we were suddenly interrupted by a cheerful voice calling from next-door.

'Hi! Hello, you two — I thought I recognised the voices. Can I come round?' and I looked up to see Janine sitting cross-legged on top of the dividing wall, looking so much like a Cornish pixie that I laughed out loud and the moment of tension evaporated.

'Janine!' I waved a hand. 'Of course, come on. Can you jump down all right from there?'

She gave a wriggle, grabbed the overhanging branch of a nearby tree and landed lightly on the grass on our side.

With a grin she joined us, flopping down on the grass at my feet.

'How's Ruby?' she asked.

'Not bad,' I replied, as Greg stared out over the garden and said nothing.

'I can't get over you two both being related to her,' Janine added, staring at Greg who seemed to be miles away, then back to me with raised eyebrows and an enquiring look. Presumably she'd sensed the atmosphere and was wondering what was going on.

'I'm glad she's coping,' she replied. 'If there's anything I can do to help, let me know.'

'Ginny, there was something I came to tell you.' She rolled over and sat up with a broad grin on her face.

My eyes widened as I said, 'Oh?' and

waited expectantly.

'I bumped into John down at the headquarters and he said to tell you that the seal you found is almost well again — and that they've called her Virginia after you!'

'Oh, that's wonderful!' I laughed happily and turned to Greg to include him in the moment, but apart from a faint smile which didn't reach his eyes, his face was impassive.

Just then we heard Ruby's voice calling for Greg from inside the house, and he pulled himself together and rose to his feet.

★ ★ ★

'What's up with him?' Janine asked as soon as he was out of earshot. 'Was it something I said?'

'Of course not, don't be silly.' I smiled and went on, 'No — you'll never believe this, Jan — I can hardly believe it myself but — '

I told her the whole story and she

210

listened round-eyed until I came to the end.

'So *that's* why he's looking so awkward,' she said. 'Oh, Ginny, that's wonderful news, isn't it? I'm so *glad* he knows the truth at last. Has he apologised to you?'

She picked a dandelion clock and idly blew the seeds away like a child.

'Not yet,' I conceded, 'but I think he was maybe getting around to it when you called.'

Janine looked stricken and jumped to her feet.

'Oh, sorry — I chose the wrong moment there, didn't I?'

I shook my head in denial.

'No, no, don't worry — it won't do him any harm to think about it for a while. By the way,' I added with a grin, 'Ruby won't thank you for sowing dandelions in her flower bed, you know.'

'Oops, sorry!' She giggled. 'Anyway, according to this dandelion, it's three o'clock, and I must get to the shop before it closes for Sunday hours, else I shan't eat tonight. Let me know if there are any further developments, Ginny. You can always give me a shout, you know.'

She grabbed the tree again and hauled herself neatly up, waving from the top of the wall then dropping with an audible thud on the other side.

★   ★   ★

Shortly after Janine had gone, Greg reappeared with a clutch of letters in his hand, waving them at me as he drew nearer.

'Aunt Ruby wants these posted. Will you come down to the box with me, Ginny? Can you manage to walk on that knee?' His face was expressionless and I nodded, recognising the invitation as an olive branch.

'OK,' I replied, rising. 'It's only a few hundred yards, and anyway, your magic ointment seems to have done it a lot of good.'

Greg smiled faintly and nodded.

'Great. I told you it was good stuff, didn't I?'

★ ★ ★

We strolled down the hill in silence and posted the letters, then Greg drew me across the main road to a seat which overlooked a large tidal pool.

'You'd better have a rest before we go back — that hill is steeper than it looks,' he said.

The tide was ebbing and a couple of swans were gliding on their stately way in the middle where the channel ran deepest, while a crowd of other water birds whose names were completely unknown to me strutted and pecked about in the rich mud left by the receding water.

I was watching a stiff-legged pure white wader with a plumy crest picking its slow and dignified way over the rocky bank below our feet, and Greg must have seen me following its progress.

'An egret,' he said, just as if I'd spoken. Then, pointing a finger towards a grassy island further away, he said, 'There's a group of curlews, see? And the busy little ones over there are dab-chicks.'

I murmured some reply as Greg, still gazing out over the pool, took a breath and then spoke in a gruff voice.

'Ginny, I don't know how to put this, but I owe you an enormous apology. I made the most monumental mistake, and I'm sorry, sorry, sorry. Truly I am. I've been all sorts of a fool. I took the situation at face value and came to all the wrong conclusions.'

'Yes,' I replied bluntly, not making it any easier for him, 'you did.'

Greg half turned towards me and laid a hand on my arm as our eyes met.

'I can only say how much I wish I could take it all back and we could start again,' he said and added earnestly, 'Ginny, do you think you could ever bring yourself to forgive me?'

I looked away and over to the

sand-hills which rose to the skyline on the far side of the pool.

'I was bitterly hurt that night, Greg,' I replied slowly, 'more hurt than you'll ever know. I felt in exactly the same position as my mother must have done years ago, and I understood exactly what she must have gone through.'

I followed the leisurely progress of a couple of gulls who flapped by overhead on their way to the sea.

'It made me realise the immensity of her suffering. The poor woman was thrown into jail because no-one would believe her, however much she swore she was innocent. And suddenly I knew how that felt.'

I looked at him again. 'And I think that was at the back of your mind that evening as well, wasn't it? Like mother, like daughter, you thought, didn't you?'

Greg's face reddened a little as he looked down at his hands, but he didn't deny it.

'And since then I've had to live with that,' I went on. 'Fortunately I had one good friend who has stood by me.'

Greg's eyebrows rose and he met my eyes.

'Janine is the only person who believed my story,' I said simply, 'and that's partly because she had her own suspicions of Lisa. Again, she couldn't prove it either, but her support meant a lot to me.'

I paused and let him take this in.

Then, having given him such a hard time, I relented.

'But time goes on and we have to go forward with it, Greg. I'm not the sort to bear a grudge for ever, so yes, I guess I could try to forgive you.'

Then I slowly shook my head and I looked down into my lap to hide a mist of sudden tears.

'But don't ask me to forget as well — not just yet.'

'Oh, Ginny, thank you, *thank you so much*.' Greg seized my hand and squeezed it hard, sending shock waves through my system and cutting short the tears before they had a chance to fall.

'I can't tell you what that means to me,' he murmured.

A small silence fell as he replaced my hand in my lap.

★　★　★

I'm not trying to excuse myself in any way,' he eventually said slowly, 'but for years I'd been blinded by Lisa's seeming love for me, and apparent sincerity. She was there for me at a very difficult time, after the accident. I have to give her some credit and admit that she really helped me get through that.

'But on the other hand, I never imagined that she had any kind of agenda going on. I never realised how two-faced and devious she really is.' he sighed and shook his head. 'She seemed so convincing, but actually she had me right where she wanted me — in her pocket.'

'Ginny, how could I have been so stupid and so blind?' He spread his hands wide with a bewildered expression on his face. 'I made a perfect fool of myself,' he finished wearily.

He looked like a hurt small boy, and my heart went out to him.

'No, Greg, you weren't stupid,' I said firmly. 'It's just that you're so straightforward and honest yourself that you expect other people to be the same.'

'You're right. I believed every word she said, right up until the day of the barbecue and the party,' he said sadly. 'Then I felt as if a window had opened, and at last I saw through her and realised that she meant nothing more to me than any of my other friends. And I told her so.'

Ah, I thought — that was in the cave when I had overheard them.

He shook his head and sighed again.

'She didn't like it, of course, and anyway, I think she'd already seen something that I hadn't even realised myself. She knew that she was going to lose me — because I was falling in love with you, Ginny.'

The sun seemed to tilt sideways and slip down the sky as my head reeled, and I wondered if I'd heard correctly.

I was speechless as Greg took both of my hands in his big, warm ones and our eyes met and locked.

'So that's why she set out to discredit you by planting the necklace. And she almost got away with it, too. I'll never forgive myself for being fooled by her . . . '

I gave a huge sigh and all the hurt, frustration and hopelessness melted away as my head slipped on to his shoulder and then I was in his arms. It felt the natural place to be and I sighed again as total happiness wrapped itself around me as surely as his embrace.

'It's in the past now, Greg. We all make mistakes. Look at me and Phil! The important thing is to learn from them, and not to let them taint the happiness that we've found. Because, you see, Greg, I love you too.'

He looked at me in wonder, and then our lips met . . .

I had come home at last and this was where I was going to stay, whatever the future might bring.

FALSE PRETENCES

Phyllis Humphrey

When Ginger Maddox, a San Francisco stock-broker, meets handsome Neil Cameron, she becomes attracted to him. But then mysterious things begin to happen, involving Neil's aunts. After a romantic weekend with Neil, Ginger overhears a telephone conversation confirming her growing suspicions that he's involved in illegal trading. She's devastated, fearing that this could end their relationship. But it's the elderly aunts who help show the young people that love will find a way.

CUCKOO IN THE NEST

Joyce Johnson

On his deathbed, reclusive million-aire Sir Harry Trevain asks his beloved granddaughter, Daisy, to restore harmony to their fractured family. But as the Trevain family gathers for Sir Harry's funeral, tensions are already surfacing. Then, at the funeral, a handsome stranger arrives from America claiming to be Sir Harry's grandson. The family is outraged, but Daisy, true to her promise to her grandfather, wel-comes the stranger to Pencreek and finds herself irresistibly drawn to Ben Trevain . . .

'I'LL BE THERE FOR YOU'

Chrissie Loveday

Amy returns home to find the house deserted and her father mysteriously absent. Her oldest friend Greg rallies round and they begin their mission to find her father. Had her father planned some sort of surprise holiday for her? Or was there a sinister purpose behind the mysterious phone calls? Mystery, adventure, possible danger and a trip to Southern Spain follow. But how could they enjoy the beautiful settings with such threats hanging over them?

JANE I'M-STILL-SINGLE JONES

Joan Reeves

Despite her ownership of a successful business in New York, Jane Louise Jones is nervous about her impending high school reunion in Vernon, Louisiana. There she must wear a badge emblazoned with her unmarried status, which Morgan Sherwood might see. Unbelievably handsome and now rich, Morgan had broken her heart in the senior year. Meanwhile, Morgan plans to make her fall in love with him all over again, he's never forgotten their passionate kisses — and now he wants more . . .

THE BAKER'S APPRENTICE

Valerie Holmes

Molly Mason dreams of escaping from the suffocating existence of life with her stepmother, Mrs Cecily Creswell and her daughter Juniper. She plans to make her escape by becoming an apprentice to her friend the local baker, Alice Arndale. However, when Juniper's fiancé Lt Cherry, a war hero, returns home early, he arrives with Mr Julian Creswell, a missing soldier, presumed dead — and Julian brings with him suspicions of murder, mystery and the key to Molly's heart . . .